Copyright 2015 by Rachel Caid. A

Cover by All by Design - http://kristi609.wix.com/allbydesign

No part of this book may be reproduced in any written, electronic, recording, or photocopying without written permission of the publisher or author. The exception would be in the case of brief quotations embodied in the critical articles or reviews and pages where permission is specifically granted by the publisher or author.

Although every precaution has been taken to verify the accuracy of the information contained herein, the author and publisher assume no responsibility for any errors or omissions. No liability is assumed for damages that may result from the use of information contained within.

Healing (Finding Home Book One)

Table of Contents

Dedication 4
Chapter One 5
Chapter Two 21
Chapter Three 26
Chapter Four 30
Chapter Five 35
Chapter Six 39
Chapter Seven 48
Chapter Eight 53
Chapter Nine 63
Chapter Ten 70
Chapter Eleven 75
Chapter Twelve 80
Chapter Thirteen 91
Chapter Fourteen 100
Chapter Fifteen 110
Chapter Sixteen 125
Chapter Seventeen 129
Chapter Eighteen 142
Chapter Nineteen 148
Chapter Twenty 160
Chapter Twenty-one 171
Chapter Twenty-two 187
Chapter Twenty-three 200
Chapter Twenty-four 205
Chapter Twenty-five 209
Chapter Twenty-six 212
Chapter Twenty-seven 218
Chapter Twenty-eight 226
Chapter Twenty-nine 233
Chapter Thirty 241
Chapter Thirty-one 255

Chapter Thirty-two ……………………………….. 265
Epilogue …………………………………………. 275
Acknowledgements ……………………………. 280
About the Author ………………………………. 282
Coming Soon ……………………………………. 283

Dedication

This book is dedicated to my biggest supporter and my favorite fan, my husband.

Babe, without you this would still be handwritten in a notebook.

Chapter One

Anna

I have needed a new center piece for my store's front window for weeks, but inspiration had eluded me. That was, until this morning when my radio alarm clock went off, playing hard, alternative rock at five in the morning. I didn't wake up fast enough to take in what song played; I was too busy trying to figure out if the DJ was sadistic or genius for playing that style of music at such an early hour. The songs changed, each more energizing than the one before it. As I let each track wake me further, an image appeared in my head; an image of what my window piece should be.

It was six by the time I drank my coffee and ate my bagel and a banana. I padded downstairs to the studio, keeping my movements are quiet as possible so no one woke. My hands itched to be used. I readied myself for the few hours of work I had ahead of me. I walked along the hallway to my sanctuary, glancing at the pictures on the wall. Smiling faces plastered the walls on both sides, filling me with warmth and happiness. I paused at the last picture, giving it a light tap with my fingertips, and opened the door to my sanctuary.

I flipped on the light as I shut the door, leaned back against it, and breathed in the smell of earth around me. Once settled in my refuge, I moved across the floor, careful to not be loud. A large forest scene was hanging off the wall to my left, covering the one window; I had trouble working if someone could watch me without my knowledge. The scene was majestic, the vivid green of the leaves, the blue sky littered with wisps of white clouds, and the deep, warm brown of the tree trunks often felt inviting enough to walk through.

On the adjacent wall hung a photograph I had taken during a day trip to Folly Island. A bright sun hung high in the left corner. The ocean was a perfect mix of grays, greens, and blues, with waves tipped in white foam. Folly Beach looked to be the perfect place for a noonday nap, warm and secluded. We lived just over thirty minutes away from some of South Carolina's most stunning beaches and that had its benefits. Spillover tourists that shopped in my store, Kiln Me Now, had helped us become popular in a relatively short time.

I moved with purpose, grabbing the clay I needed for my new project and the regular stock that needed to be replaced. I hoped to get done with the vases today; the sculpted leaves needed wait until I replenished more of the regular stock. I placed my tools within an easy reach on a small rolling table to my right and my bucket of water sat in front of the wheel. I picked my playlist, pushed in my earbuds, and pressed play, ready to begin.

Music filled me. I moved with the beat of the drums. My mind became lost in the screaming guitar. Linkin Park's "Guilty All the Same" blasting in my ears – my go to driving force. I kept the volume loud, blocking out the rest of the world. The only thing I could see are my hands, covered in cool water and brown clay, my movements careful, strategic, and with just the right pressure to create the height and width I needed.

I got in my zone, the soft clay moving beneath my hands, the aroma of it filling my nose. The image in my head came to life before my eyes, pushing me. I worked without stopping for over an hour and a half. As I pushed the clay for the last plate which I was making flatter, flaying out at the edges, the lamp next to the door caught my eye when it flickered, signaling I had a visitor. It was most likely my younger sister, Christine, coming to say good morning after eating breakfast with Roman.

The lamp had been wired to a switch on the other side of the door, a trick we had created together after she caught me by surprise while I was working, oblivious to anything but music and clay; clay she ended up wearing. As funny as it was, I hated to waste the clay and Christine didn't want to worry over ruining her clothes every time she needed me while I was back here.

She walked across the room, her long legs covered in soft gray yoga pants, topped with a loose, pink tee shirt. Her wavy, chestnut hair swayed as she moved. Christine and I looked similar, as sisters do, but her face formed a perfect heart with soft cheeks and nose, whereas mine was longer, with sharper features. Our eyes, though, they were the same deep brown with flecks of gold.

I tilted my head to give her easier access to the wires so she could pull the earbuds out, allowing me to keep working. Christine smiled brightly at me, "Hey Anna-banana, Roman is eating those pastries that Mrs. Maloney had her niece bring over yesterday. I swear that woman would keep him if she thought you'd let her. She might not wait for permission if he keeps winking at her every time we walk in or out of the bakery."

I chuckled to myself, "Oh, she'd give him back when he got tired and cranky, don't you think?"

She nodded her agreement and then shifted her focus to my new pieces. "Hey Anna, these are different. What are you going to do with them? They aren't our usual stock vases."

I explained my idea of a collage of vases connected with sculpted, interlocking leaves and the excitement was obvious in her voice. "This is really going to draw a crowd. And what perfect timing, with your enrolment form for our pottery class going up soon, people will be over the moon to learn how to do this, they always are. So," she paused, pursing her lips to the side, unsure of what to say, "are you going to let me sell this one? Or is it going to be donated too?"

With my attention still on my work, which I had taken my time to form a simple column of clay into a curved vase, I tried to give her an offended look. But Christine was right, I loved my showpieces and prefer to find them a loving home than let a stranger buy them. My expression disintegrated as I slid my eyes over to her, catching her peering at me with careful consideration. I laughed, and then explained, "I don't know. I want to keep it for a while though and show it off until I let you convince me to sell it. It will be perfect for the window, and I hoped, someone's home or office one day." I paused, trimming the last bits off of the plate. "Just give me some time to get this done and clean up and I'll be out."

Christine nodded her approval and started out the door. "I'll give you 30 minutes, and then I'm sending Roman in to get you," she shouted over her shoulder. Knowing that could end in disaster, I focused my energy into carving small ridges into the clay, deciding at the last minute I was making a decorative tray and finished with only moments to spare.

I was filling my bucket with warm water, ready to clean my tools and counter space, when I heard quick footsteps thundering the length of the hall towards my studio door. Seconds later, Roman came barreling in, wide smile splayed across his perfect face, eyes gleaming with mischief. "Christine said I could tell you to get your butt in gear! Move it woman, we hafta do stuff! The store is opening soon and you're dirty."

I took a few seconds to compose myself, taking a few calming breaths before I placed my hand on his chin and gave a gentle tug to angle his head so he looked me in the eyes. I gathered my patience before answering him. "Roman Henry Johnston, you will not tell me to 'get my butt in gear,' you will not call me 'woman,' and lastly, you will open your arms and give your Momma a proper hug and kiss before we start this day."

His sweet smile never left his face as his tiny arms opened wide, enveloping me as best he could, smacking my cheek with a loud, wet kiss. When he pulled away he had enough sense to try to appear sheepish, but couldn't quite pull it off. "Sorry Momma, I'll go make sure the shelves are dusted. I'm going to earn my dollar before you get done!" Roman ran out of the room, off to find his dusting rag and earn his money. It amazed me how much motivation the dollar a day I paid inspired my five year old son.

I watched the door for a few seconds after he disappeared before I finished my clean up ritual. Once I finished, I moved swiftly back upstairs. I needed to shower, change my clothes, and open the store for the day.

I was just finishing up blow drying my hair when Roman came into my bedroom through the bathroom we shared. He always wanted to "help" apply my makeup; though his color choice left much to be desired. This morning I got lucky, though, and the only thing he wanted was to sit with me as I got ready.

As he took a seat on his bright green bean bag next to me at the thrift store vanity, the morning inquisition started. "Momma, what time is Unca Pete coming today? Is he gonna move stuff for you? 'Cause I can help. Can I help some customers today? What are we gonna have for lunch?" Roman fired off question after question faster than I could edge in a word. No matter how many times in the past I had tried to get him to take a breath, he couldn't seem to stop until his thoughts were out. I leaned back and waited until the end to answer.

"Well, Uncle Pete has made a point to come in to see if we need help around ten o'clock." I had noticed that my brother Pete had come in like clockwork at ten after a week or so, and after mentioning it to Christine, and being the caring sisters we are, we had to investigate. From what I gathered, Mrs. Maloney had sent her niece—her very pretty niece—to make a few of her deliveries, and we suspected Pete was trying to bump into her. "And, you know, he has to help us move heavy things. It makes him feel strong. And we want Uncle Pete to feel strong." Flexing my arms, I gave him a conspiratorial wink, and he broke out into a fit of giggles.

"Now, go on down and see if Aunt Christine needs you for anything before we open. Once she's done with you, you might find a brand new pad of paper and crayons in my top left dr-." I was cut off by Roman's excited shriek piercing my ears. I knew my little budding artist would love his surprise.

Roman jumped up and down then dashed out of the room, shouting "Aunt Chris, you don't need me do you?" I smiled to myself, knowing Christine liked to let him get away with a quick chore before letting him go. One last quick brush of my long, brown hair and I was on my way downstairs to open for the day.

***

We had been open a few hours when Pete opened the door. He was still laughing towards his favorite delivery girl who I could still see through the window. "When are you going to bite the bullet and ask her out?" I asked him the same question at least twice a week. His face was deadpan before walking up and tweaking my nose, hard. "Damn it Pete!" I shouted, smacking him on the arm. "That hurts and you know it." I drew my eyebrows together, shooting daggers at him with my eyes.

He gave a soft chuckle, shaking his head, letting his shaggy hair shift over his forehead, "Sis, you've got to quit butting into my business. If I ask Alex on a date, it'll be between me and her. Get that through your thick head."

"So it's Alex, huh? I never get to introduce myself since you steal her attention at every chance. Anyway, I worked up vases this morning and I need my big, strong, amazing brother to help me move them to the upper drying rack. Do you have time to do it?" I batted my eyelashes at him to add drama, holding my clasped hands under my chin.

Pete just shook his head and headed towards the door at the back on the store. Just as his hand touched the knob, the door burst open, and Pete was plowed into by Roman. "Whoa! Slow down Rome, you almost knocked me out with the door, dude."

Roman just stared up at his uncle, his bright smile never wavering, "Uncle Pete, you're too strong for anyone to knock out, silly." A short laugh slipped out of my mouth before I got it covered with my hand. Pete slid his eyes sideways at me before asking Roman, "Does your Mom give you lessons?"

Roman looked at him, eyebrows drawn together, confused. "Lessons for what?"

Pete just laughed and picked him up, throwing him over his shoulder as if he was a sack of potatoes, making Roman squeak with laughter. He started back on his way to the studio. "Does she give you lessons on how to work me, boy? Because you sound just like she did at your age." Pete's shoulders shook with laughter. "You comin' or what, Sis? Or do you want Rome and me to do it by ourselves?" He called over his shoulder. I put the pen in my hand on the counter and followed them.

"Where do you want them?" Pete asked as he lifted the first vase. I pointed to the second rack from the ceiling, with an innocent smile. "Of course you do, Banana. I'll get them there, but just 'cause I love you." He shook his head at me and got to work, listening as I explained the new piece.

"Oh, I am so excited to get this done. No matter what, it will be great." I've been working as a potter for about six years, but I was still learning techniques, perfecting my style as I went. "It's going to be awesome when it's finished, Pete, my best yet." I soaked in the sight, seeing it completed in my head. I expected it to be a powerful draw in the window.

Pete broke into my thoughts asking Roman, "So, Little Dude, what do you say to a trip for ice cream this afternoon when I get back from my meeting? I expect I deserve some after my hard work and I need company." The wide eyes directed at me begged for permission. With a quick nod to both of them, Roman ran out to tell Christine his new plans.

"You spoil him, Pete. And I love you for it."

"He's not being spoiled, Anna. The boy needs time with a man, and until you quit getting after me to date and go out on one of your own, I'm volunteering. I love hanging out with my Little Dude, and he loves it too. I need to get in there while I'm still the coolest guy he knows. Not that I'm worried," he added with a wink, trying to bring some humor into the conversation. His brutal honesty shocked me. Most of the time, we skate around the whole issue of dating, something neither of us put much effort into it. We each had our reasons, and while my family knew mine, Pete kept his to himself. But, since I had brought it up first, I let his comment roll off of my back.

With a nod, I motioned for us to leave the studio. "I need to get back to work. Call me before you come and I'll make sure Roman is up from his nap."

As we walked through the storefront, Pete stopped and spun to face me. "Kid needs a Dad, Anna. It's been a long time, you can't hide forever." With a gentle kiss to my forehead, Pete turned and walked out of the store, leaving me stunned.

"He's not wrong, you know." I jumped, taken by surprise from behind.

"Mom! I didn't know you were stopping by today. What's up?" I tried for chipper, but the her frown proved I had missed the mark.

"Anna, honey, I'll let it go for now, but he isn't wrong." She took a breath that was a little sad and a lot frustrated before continuing. "I came to see if you and Christine would like to go out to dinner tonight, just us girls. I want to try that new Italian place that just opened. Your father doesn't want to go. What do you think? I'll even throw in an overnight babysitting by Grandpa and me."

My mother's eyes narrowed and her chin gave a slight tilt to the left, daring me to decline. This was more than a request. She needed this, and I was happy to do it. "You've got a deal, Mom. I think we could use a night out. Christine has been talking about going to Fritz's for a while anyway. We can go there for drinks later."

My Mom smiled at me, "Thanks honey. I need to get out with my girls. I'll see you at seven?" with a nod, I gave her a hug. We said our goodbyes, and I went back to working on the order I had on the counter.

It was ten minutes before seven that evening, Christine and I had changed in record time after closing up for the day. Neither of us wanted to make Mom wait; or worse, help pick out our clothes. I had chosen a pair of dark-wash skinny jeans, paired with dark brown suede knee-high boots, topped with a bright paisley peasant blouse. I had left my long hair loose and cascading down my back, a relaxed yet put together image. Christine, on the other hand, had gone all out. She was excited to go out to Fritz's after dinner and had pulled out all the stops. She was decked out in a short, metallic purple skirt, a fitted cowl-necked, black sleeveless shirt, and a pair of silver strappy heels. We certainly made quite the pair.

"Are you girls ready to go?" Mom called with a hint of impatience from the door to the stairwell.

"We're on our way right now! Anna, grab my bag please?" Christine shouted, half to Mom, half at me.

We made our way downstairs and out the door to my Jeep. It was an old 1987 Cherokee Laredo, but Pete's mechanic helped keep it running. As I slid into the driver's seat, mom opened the passenger door and Christine made her way into the back seat. As I started the engine, I looked over and smiled, "Thanks for dinner tonight, Mom. We could both use the break. And thanks for keeping Roman for the night. It will be nice to hang out with Chris and not have to worry about bedtime." She gave me a knowing smile, but said nothing. She'd raised three rambunctious kids of her own, she understood.

When we got to the restaurant, Rinaldi's was only half filled with diners, but they appeared to enjoy their meals. The three of us followed the hostess to a nice corner booth, placed our wine orders, and pursued the menu. When the waitress came with our drinks, we ordered and relaxed into our wine. "So, who's Pete's new girl?" Mom asked, flitting her eyes between Christine and me with suspicion.

"What are you talking about?" I asked, shocked by her accusation.

"What new girl?" Christine sat in silence for a moment and then you it was as if I saw the light bulb go off over her head, she rattled off the gossip like a machine gun, "OH! You mean Mrs. Maloney's niece, don't you? Well, she moved into the apartment over the bakery a few months ago. I haven't really had a chance to meet her though. Pete makes a point of running into her nearly every day, but he hasn't asked her out. Chicken, I guess."

With a sad shake of her head, Mom shifted her attention. "What about you, Anna? Peter is right; you need to get out there. Not just for Roman, but for yourself. You have so much love to give, Honey, and it'd be a shame to waste it."

"I'm not wasting it, Mom. I'm giving it to Roman. He is the only man I need in my life. Between him, you guys, and the store, my life is pretty darn full. I'm good, Mom, I swear." My eyes pleased with her to let it go. I wanted her to stop worrying about me, as I was living a fulfilling life, and I was doing it without a man. I couldn't do it to myself again, and I certainly couldn't do it to Roman. He would get attached, like any normal kid, and if, no, when it ended, he'd be devastated. God, what if he blamed himself? It was too much to ask of a little boy; I couldn't.

"One of these days Roman will be all grown up, Banana. Who will you hide behind then?" My eyes shot to Christine, wondering why she was adding to this. She was aware of what I had dealt with years ago; it had been her shoulder I had cried on the most. The murmuring of the surrounding diners disappeared as I stared slack-jawed at my sister. Before I had the chance to respond, the waitress returned with our food, saving me from anymore of this attack.

We ate in silence for a few minutes. The food was excellent. I had ordered chicken parmesan, a longtime favorite of mine. The chicken was cooked to perfection; covered with a light, crispy coating of panko crumbs, smothered in a deep red marinara that was so flavorful, I wanted to eat it by itself. I ripped a piece from the loaf of bread in front of me, dipped it into the sauce, and savored the bite. It was so good, a quiet moan escaped my lips, but I didn't care.

"That must be some sauce." I spun around, startled by the voice behind me, even more shocked to find myself eye level with the owner of the voice's crotch. My eyes drifted up taking in the picture, dark jeans gave way to a faded AC/DC tee shirt. I kept scanning up the six foot solid wall of man until I reached his face. His square jaw was softened by a smirk as his blue eyes danced with humor. "I think I'm gonna have to order whatever you got, if it tastes that good," he said, chuckling slightly. I was broken out of my stupor, and managed a sideway glance at my sister, who was staring, slack-jawed and wide-eyed. Knowing that expression and at once drew attention to her.

"Well, maybe you should ask my sister here what she got, I bet she'd even let you try it." I winked at him, proud that I had stayed blush free and keep my voice even and light.

Christine shook her head to clear her thoughts and blessed the visitor with her brilliant smile. "Well of course you can have a taste. Here, let me blow on it, it is a bit hot."

They flirted back and forth for a while, but I was too annoyed at everyone for attacking me, just because I don't date, to pay attention. After a few minutes, the hostess handed our visitor's to-go order to him and he was on his way.

Determined to enjoy the evening, I forced the negative thoughts away. We chatted about nothing important, just enjoying each other's company. When the bill came, we all three scrambled for it, but Mom got there first; as always. "You've got to be quick if you want to treat me, girls. I enjoy doting on you, you know." Christine and I shared a silent conversation, but didn't argue. There wasn't any point.

With dinner done, we drove mom home. Christine and I wished Roman good night. "Now, be good for Grandma and Grandpa tonight, baby. I want a good report in the morning." I pulled him in for a big hug and kiss. He held me for a few moments, but decided it was time to let go and harass Grandma for some cookies.

As he ran off he yelled back, "Bye, Mom. Love you!" I looked up at my father, smiling.

"Thanks for tonight, Dad. He loves sleepovers with you."

"I do too, Banana, I do too." He gave me a squeeze on the shoulder, as usual, held my eye for a moment and opened the front door for us.

Healing (Finding Home Book One)

With quick goodbyes, we were out and in the Jeep, ready for a much needed sister's night out.

Chapter Two

Anna

We arrived at Fritz's bar just after nine. The lot was three quarters full, a comment occurrence on summer nights like tonight, promising us a crowd. As I opened the front door the familiar smell of our favorite hangout invited me in. The mix of sawdust, beer, and frying oil, was a hug from an old friend; the scent filled me, offering me immediate relaxation. I dropped my shoulders an inch, took in a deep breath, and smiled. Christine relaxed as soon as we entered; the need for our night out becoming obvious. As we walked, her hips moved absently to the soft music pumping from the old jukebox. Fritz didn't like having to shout to be heard, and so the music was loud once in a while, when he would have a local band play live. It made this the perfect place to hang out and catch up.

We walked over to the bar, grabbing the bartender's attention. Behind the bar was Casey, Fritz's youngest son. He had gone to school with us, just a year behind Christine. His sandy blonde hair, in desperate need of a trim, was falling into his eyes when he glanced up at us. With a quick wave, he grabbed two bottles of Miller Lite, ripped the tops off with ease, and walked over, ignoring everyone else.

"Anna," he said with a nod, "Christine, good to see you ladies tonight. We've got specials if you're hungry." He pointed at the chalkboard behind the bar. "And a couple of guys new to town on the pool table if you're itchin' for a game." Casey handed the bottles to us with an ornery smile. He loved watching Christine and I hustle guys at pool.

It always took a while for them to catch on; they never think that two chicks are good enough to be sharks. Only once had it gotten ugly because the guys we played just can't lose to a girl, but Fritz and Casey took care of the situation. "Nothing a shotgun pointin' at your face can't fix," had been Fritz's motto, and he wasn't wrong.

"Maybe later Case, Anna and I need to unwind before we break out the welcome wagon," Christine replied with a flirtatious smile before pushing off of the bar to find a seat. We made our way across the sawdust covered floor until we found an empty table. We took in the Saturday night crowd, both leaning into the backs of our stools, and enjoyed the scene with ice-cold beer.

"Fancy seeing you here," a somewhat familiar man's voice said from behind me. Christine's brows shot up in surprise for a split second, but she hid it quickly. A slow, flirtatious smile spread across her face, eyes lighting up at whoever was there. I eyed her with suspicion before taking my time turning around in my seat. When my eyes shifted from Christine to our visitor, I realized he was the same man from the restaurant. Giving a friendly smile, I motioned an invitation for him to join us, knowing there would be no argument from my sister.

"So, did you follow me here or is it fate?" he asked me with a smirk.

I gave a small smile, bringing the chilled, brown bottle to my lips, taking a long pull of beer, "Must be fate. Christine, you're a big believer of fate, aren't you?" I asked, drawing attention back to her. I could tell by the way she was breathing, as if she had to remember to do it, that she was really into this guy. She picked up the queue and drew him close, leaning in for a private discussion. I directed an appreciative smile at them before scanning the room. There was a mix of locals and tourists filling the space, I spotted a few friends across the way and gave a wave of hello. It wasn't enough to encourage, but enough to still be friendly. I didn't want to share my sister tonight. I glanced over at our visitor; well not much.

"So, Anna, what do you think?" Christine's question broke me out of my thoughts, and I turned to her with a questioning look. "Think about what, Chris?" She shook her head, and glanced over at her new friend, "Oh Craig, don't mind her, she gets lost in her head sometimes. Anna, Craig here was saying he might want to sign up for your next pottery class. Isn't that fantastic? And he has a friend," she said with a toothy grin aimed right at me. I grimaced at her, but as I did, Craig's smile faltered slightly; he must have thought it was regarding him taking my class and not Christine's obvious matchmaking scheme.

I cleared my through, causing him to raise his eyes to my own, and smiled with sincerity. I tried to put him at ease, "Craig, I would love for you to come to my class, but be warned, it can make you hungry. You might want to have plans to eat right afterward." Ha! Take that

Christine. Surprise registered on his face first, then his lips formed a mischievous smile as he looked me straight in the eye and asked, "So, will you be free?"

I choked on the sip of beer I had just taken, shocked that he had asked me, when he burst out laughing. Tilting his head toward my sister, he said, "You're right, she's perfect." My eyes darted between the two as they shared an inside joke. How they had one after just fifteen minutes is beyond me, but to be truthful, I hadn't been paying attention. Christine smacked his arm playfully and with no reservations she schooled her features, before asking Craig in a dramatic, yet sultry voice, "Wanna go to dinner after class, big boy?"

"Of course I do, but I might not be able to wait that long, how about we go out Tuesday night for dinner? I can see if Noah's free and we can make it a foursome," Craig offered with hope filled eyes. I hated to be the downer, but I couldn't go out again so soon. Roman can't spend all of his time at his grandparents' house. Christine knew my dilemma and saved me from having to make up an excuse. "Oh, Anna can't go that night. She'll be busy going over inventory, but I would love to." She flashed him an irresistible smile, and both seemed to forget about me for a moment, but not long enough.

Craig twisted his neck around, scanning the floor for someone, "Noah should be around here somewhere, I thought he was just going to grab a couple beers and find me." He turned back to us, "Don't go anywhere, I will go find him and get you two introduced." Without waiting for a response, he lifted himself off of the stool and disappeared into the crowd.

Chapter Three

Noah

How do I always get talked into this shit? Craig owes me for coming out tonight. I'm here against my better judgment because he met some chick at the restaurant when he picked up our dinner. I would have made him make a drive-thru run instead of getting real food if I had known I'd end up playing wingman when he decided we haven't been out enough since moving here. We've been up since five, planning the remodel we were starting. After staring in the mirror for a minute, I scrubbed my hands over my face. I held them there for just a minute when Craig's voice boomed with laughter from behind me. I lifted my eyes to meet his in the mirror.

"Are you hiding like a little girl, man? Hurry up and get out there, you won't regret it. Christine's sister came, and she is exactly what you need. Move it, I don't want them to get distracted."

"I'm coming, shit, give me a break. You've got another thirty minutes, but after that I'm out of here. I'm beat, brother."

"You won't be saying that when you see her."

I grabbed the side of the bathroom's wooden door and made my way out behind Craig. He's been trying to get me to go out for a while. After my breakup with Kiersten, I wasn't really up for it. I got my needs met, but the girls knew the score up front – nothing serious. I didn't want serious yet, so why Craig was pushing me towards the sister of the girl he's interested in made little sense. Sisters stick together.

Craig zigzagged through the crowd which looked thicker than when I left. Damn, how long was I in there? I grabbed a couple beers from the bar on my way over since it would be weird if I had just been hanging out in the bathroom, so I tried to keep an eye on where he went. I lost him for a second, but found him standing at a tall table with two girls and walked up from behind, offering him a bottle.

I eyed the girl across the table from where I was standing, wondering which one she was. She was good-looking, but a bit on the skinny side for me. Besides, the way she looked at Craig, I figured she must be his new focus. She smiled at him and turned her attention to me. "Hi, you must be Noah," she said, cheerfully. "I'm Christine, and this lovely lady is my sister, Anna," She waved her hand towards the girl next to where Craig was standing.

As she turned to face me, I stopped breathing. The curtain of dark hair framed her face, a deep contrast to her pale skin. He cheeks flushed pink, making me wonder if it was the beer in her hand or me causing it. I moved my eyes up, hoping I was acting more casual than I felt, and my reward was a set of deep brown eyes, flecked with gold, staring right back at me. I swore I saw her breath catch in her throat, but that may have been wishful thinking. I cleared my throat, and my thoughts, I extended my hand to her, "Noah Evans, pleasure to meet you."

She extended her hand, and as soon as we touched I swear the heat of her slender fingers straight to my groin. I almost jerked my hand away in surprise, but thankfully I held firm. We held each other's eyes for a moment, and as hers widened a fraction, I knew she was affected too. She motioned for me to sit down and I didn't hesitate, taking the stool next to her, I leaned over, brushing my arm against hers. I figured a little contact couldn't hurt, but when she made a subtle shift away, I found out I was wrong.

"So, what are you guys up to tonight?" Christine asked, eyes flitting between me and Craig. "Seems like you could have just eaten here, don't you think?"

Craig chimed in before I could respond. "Well, 'ole Noah here gets a bit growly if he's not fed on time, so I ordered us some dinner closer to the house we're working on. I didn't think he'd make it through the rest of the night if he had to wait," he said with a laugh.

Anna was smiling, still listening to us, but not looking at us – she was watching the crowd. I decided if she wasn't comfortable, I wasn't going to push it. I didn't want to date anyone anyway. I shifted in my seat, giving Anna more room, and joined the conversation in front of me. "Hey, I might get testy, but I bought your dinner, so quit complaining. Christine, don't listen to him, he's just sore because we have a demo day tomorrow, and there'll be a lot of heavy lifting. It wounds him that his little girly arms can't keep up with me."

"Now don't you go listening to him, ladies, he doesn't compare to me," Craig said as he lifted his arms to flex. The guy was big, but in no way bigger than me. Well, I hadn't checked the ways he could be bigger, but I was pretty sure I'd win. "Tomorrow is going to be a ball buster of a day, right Noah? This is one of the biggest remodels we've taken on in a long time. Sure will look good when it's done though." Craig turned to Christine and asked, "So, what do you ladies do?"

Christine answered immediately, her hands moving in her normal, animated way, "Well, the artistic genius next to you owns the pottery store here in Franklin and I help her run it. She creates amazing plates, cups, vases, and oh, you should see some of her elaborate candlesticks, those seriously rock. I push the pencil in the office and keep the numbers straight, but it's Anna who draws a crowd." The warmth in Christine's face as she spoke about her sister said even more than her words. "I was so happy when she finally decided to open her shop. I quit my job and never looked back. Anna is an amazing boss; I'm lucky really."

"She exaggerates, as I'm sure you figured out for yourselves," Anna said with a slightly annoyed tone. I slid my eyes over towards her, finding her beautiful face twisted in a scowl at her sister. It was interesting to learn that she doesn't take compliments well. "I am no better than anyone else. She just wants me to let her off work early Tuesday for a hot date. Right chickie?" The scowl changed with a slight twitch of her lips, a smile she wasn't ready to let loose yet. Damn, that

Healing (Finding Home Book One)

was a shame; for some reason I really wanted to see another one of her smiles.

Chapter Four

Anna

I'm pretty sure Chris knows I'm going to kill her for that over the top portrayal. I take my work seriously, and yes, I have talent, but bragging is not something I have ever felt comfortable doing. Even less so with Noah right next to me making me very aware of every look he gives me. My goodness, the electricity that went through me when he touched my hand almost knocked me out of my seat and into his arms. When his arm brushed against mine, I had to move away, afraid of the growing sensation at my core, all for a guy I had known for a handful of minutes. It was crazy; where was my control?

I did not expect Craig's friend to be so gorgeous. His perfect square jaw had a shadow of stubble, as if he hadn't shaved in a few days, and his eyes – those piercing blue orbs – made me forget everyone else in the bar when they met mine. His blonde hair, cut close to his scalp, was just long enough to hold onto in the throes of passion. Whoa, where did that come from? I mean, he's hot, but I'm not available. I shouldn't even be staring at him this hard, but not looking at him was impossible.

In an effort to steer the conversation, I had was an idiot and brought up Christine and Craig's date. Now I hoped they remembered I would not let them make it a foursome. It didn't take long for me to learn that it was not going my way.

"You know, since Anna can't go out and Christine would have to leave you in the lurch, Noah and I could bring dinner to you." Craig's eyes were pinned on mine, almost begging me to say yes. Why, though, I wasn't sure. They could easily go without Noah and me. He shifted his eyes to his friend, "Noah, don't you think we can make that happen?"

I panicked; I didn't have men over to my home. Well, not for me. Christine was a big girl, and it wasn't as if she dated so many men that it was a negative influence on Roman. My eyes pleaded with my sister, but I could see memories of our conversations from earlier that day written across her face. I knew what was coming, and though I didn't appreciate it, it came from a place of love and concern. I decided to deal with her later.

"Well, now, how sweet! We would be able to eat and organize the store at the same time. Anna, that gets you a list of what needs to be replaced in half the time. Then we can relax with a few beers after." She held my eyes, daring me to back out. I couldn't for two reasons; one, it would be plain rude, and two, I could tell she was really into this guy and I didn't want to be the bitchy sister.

I huffed out a breath, "Fine, but you'll need to bring an extra portion. Roman will be home, and he eats more than people think." There I said his name. I waited for the questions to start; the fact that I am a single mother, and therefore too busy to date, would now be brought to light, and Noah would be on his way. Right? Roman wasn't something I ever tried to hide. Hell no, he was everything. My family thought I used him as a shield, an excuse to not date; but that wasn't true, not completely.

"Who's Roman?" This came from Craig.

"My son." It's always been best to get this out early. It was rare for me to meet someone new, and even rarer for me to date them. This was the best way to weed out the guys that couldn't deal. I glanced between the two men, wondering what they thought; hoping one of them would bow out of dinner now. Craig gave Noah a look I couldn't decipher, and I thought I was in the clear, but Noah gave his friend a subtle nod of acceptance, and I knew dinner would happen no matter what.

"What does Roman prefer to eat? I know I was one hell of a picky kid, and I hated it when I had to eat shit that I didn't like." It was a sweet thought, and I wanted to be glad that Christine found such a nice guy, however I had to admit I felt a little defeated.

"Roman is actually less picky than his aunt here, so you might want to run the menu by her before ordering." I said while pointing a finger at Christine. Her eyes lit up, and I knew I had not only caught her by surprise, but made her night. Yup, she owed me, but right now I just wanted to let her be happy.

"Well, why don't you ladies order and tell us where to pick it up. We'll leave it to you." Christine had developed a weird control issue with food while she was in college so at that statement I knew Craig would be around for a while. Noah and Craig came as a package, I was sure, so I needed to be friendly.

Dinner on Tuesday had the serious potential to be awkward, but I didn't want to disappoint Christine. I sat back, finishing my beer. I signaled for the closest waitress and ordered another round of beer. I was going to need at least one more if I was going to make it through the rest of the night.

Chapter Five

Noah

I studied Anna out of the corner of my eye while she told us about her son. There was no way Craig had known about Roman, and I knew he was worried how it would affect me. I could tell she expected me to bail, most guys did. Hell, I could tell Craig thought I was going to as well. The thing was, I liked kids, even with my history, and knowing Anna was not only running her own business but raising a child on top of that, well, it made her even more tempting. I respected the dedication and work that went into that and putting all of that in the hot package next to me was making sticking to my "nothing serious" plan hard. Anna was making a lot of things hard.

I shifted in my seat, hoping for some relief, when Craig caught my eye. He gave me a knowing look and stifled a laugh. I wanted to keep things flowing to keep Anna comfortable, so I started to ask about Anna's store. I didn't get a word out before another girl joined our group. She was tall, blonde, and thin, the type of girl guys flock to. Compared to the sisters at our table, she reminded me of a blowup doll and instantly appeared to be about as bright as one.

"Banana, I can't believe you're out tonight! It's been forever." She all but squealed at us, drawing out the last word. I looked at Anna and mouthed "Banana" with a questioning glance. The bland one she gave right back was hilarious, and I fought back a grin. "Where is Roman tonight? Your parent's have him?" The dig was subtle, and if she would have said any of it without staring at me while slipping her hand onto my arm, she might have gotten away with it. Once her tongue slipped out to wet her lips, I was done. I hated girls like that. It was just bitchy and I don't do bitchy. This conversation was over.

I leaned back, moving my arm out from under her clutches, and slid the other one around Anna's shoulders. Pulling her close, I looked our guest in the eye, "Anna's parents were kind enough to keep him tonight so these two ladies could get a well-deserved night of relaxation." Bull's eye, her smile faltered when she realized I already knew about Roman. She mumbled something that sounded close to "that's nice" and moved away as fast as she could in her "fuck me" heels. I watched her walk away, glad to have deflected the situation. It wasn't until I realized that all I could smell was peaches that I noticed I still had my arm around Anna. She hadn't attempted to move away, so I shifted my arm lower, behind her back, resting it on the top of the stool.

Both Craig and Christine looked at my arm, faces filled with shock. Craig's I understood, but I was guessing by Christine's reaction that Anna didn't let many guys get this close. An odd feeling, a mix of pride, comfort and something I couldn't quite pin down, came over me. I decided not to analyze my thoughts and instead asked, "Who the hell was that chick? I'm guessing not a friend of yours?"

The girls nodded, eyes rolling in unison, while Christine answered, "That bitch just hates it when she doesn't get the fresh meat first." Craig was on the verge of spitting his beer on the table, but controlled it before answering. "Well, thanks for protecting us. I think she was ready to tie poor Noah in the basement." Both girls burst with laughter, but unfortunately I was now picturing Anna tied to my bed, sliding my fingers through her thick hair, and working my tongue along the curves of her neck and torso. Shit, I gotta stop. I shifted in my seat, again, and finished my beer.

Two rounds later, I glanced at my watch, "I hate to break up the party, ladies, but it's closing in on eleven and we have to be up early tomorrow to get started. Just let us know where to pick up dinner, and we'll see you, say, around 7?" I watched the reactions of our group and hoped I didn't sound like an asshole. When I shifted my focus to Anna, she looked relieved. "Oh, that's fine Noah; we really should get going too. It's rare we get the chance to stay out this late." She started to stand up, but wobbled and started to lose her balance. It was a good thing I was right there to catch her. I held onto her arm the rest of the way to the lot and didn't let go when we reached the door to her Jeep.

"Are you sure you're okay to drive? You seem a little," I hesitated not wanted to offend her. "I would be more comfortable if one of us drove you back." I turned to Craig, "You don't mind following me back to their place, do you?"

"No problem," he turned to Christine, "why don't you hop in my truck and we can discuss our plans a little more." With an eyebrow waggled and aimed at her, Christine grabbed the handle of the door, and with Craig's help hopped right in to the cab. Anna and I stood there like statues as the trucks taillights disappeared down the road.

"Well, I guess we can just meet them there." Anna said with a strained laugh. I led her to the passenger-side door and helped her get settled. I was slightly bent over as she turned to grab the seatbelt, her face landing inches from mine. My gaze dropped to her mouth just as her teeth sunk into her bottom lip. I risked a peek at her eyes and they were on my mouth, tempting me. Before I gave in to temptation, she cleared her throat and shook her head gently, breaking me out of my thoughts. I straightened, shut her door, and made my way to the driver's side.

I started the Jeep and pulled out of the parking lot, going the same direction my friend's truck had taken. After a few minutes of uncomfortable silence, Anna spoke. "You'll need to take the next right. The store is two blocks down on the left. We live right above it." She sounded tired, and I almost wished I had called it a night earlier; almost. I maneuvered into the drive next to the shop and parked.

Chapter Six

Anna

I started to open my door when Noah grabbed my hand and gave it a small squeeze. Startled, I twisted around to look at him. My breath caught in my throat at the sight. The shadows fell against his face, giving him an edgy, somewhat dangerous vibe. His sexy, full lips were pressed in a thin, aggravated line. I had to admit to myself in that moment that he was fucking hot.

"I'll get that for you. Just hang on." Noah stepped from the Jeep and made his way around the front. This gave me my first chance to take him in toe to top. His black tee shirt clung to his shoulders and chest, showing off every hill and valley his muscles created. Noah's jeans hung on his hips, hugging his perfect ass. My door opened, but I couldn't pull my eyes from Noah's body. The sound of him clearing his throat forced me out of my head and I realized I was still staring at him. My cheeks were instantly hot, and I was grateful for the late hour because the limited lighting would hide my blushed cheeks.

"Thank you, Noah. I'm just not used to having a gentleman around." I took his hand, stepped out of the Jeep, and led him around the corner to the back door. I reached in my black clutch and found my keys. When I tuned to thank Noah for the evening, I smacked into a brick wall. Ok, it was his chest, but it was rock hard and unyielding. I would have stumbled back, but Noah's arm whipped out behind me, steadying me and pulling me to him in one sweep. The aroma of pine and sawdust surrounded me as I sucked in a breath. Just as I started to lean into him, the light above the door went out, blanketing us in darkness.

"What the hell? Are they trying to hurry us up or something?" Noah asked with a nervous laugh. It was enough though, and I pushed out of his hold, coming back to my senses. I couldn't do this. It was too much.

"There's a motion detector, but it doesn't work the best." To prove my point I took a few steps around until light flooded the back yard. Back strip of grass and small porch was more accurate. I went to unlock the door, but realized Christine more than likely left it unlocked, so I twisted the knob and moved inside to the hallway.

Noah followed me up the stairs and I swear his eyes were glued to my ass the entire way. We reached the end of the staircase and I opened the door to our apartment. The living room was straight ahead of us. To the right was a wall with three doors, each to a bedroom. Mine was first, closest to the stairs for quick exits in the morning, then came Roman's. Christine's was last, overlooking the street below us. The living room had two large couches, a deep brown with thick, welcoming cushions and bright, colorful pillows. The furniture, along with a fuzzy throw rug in a similar color, complimented the light blue walls perfectly. There was a small coffee table that still had a recent drawing and a few crayons scattered across it.

    I didn't see Craig or Christine so I glanced at her door, which, to my relief, was open. I heard voices coming from the left and realized they must be in the kitchen. We moved toward the conversation, I sensed Noah's presence behind me and he kept himself close enough that the heat from his chest radiated onto my back. I bit my lip and opened and closed my fists, trying to distract myself from the effect he had on me. I couldn't remember the last time I was so aware of a man near me. Though, I wasn't sure how I felt or what I wanted to do about it. My sister would have a few suggestions for me, but I wasn't ready to hear them. Not tonight, at least. I would have to deal with her tomorrow.

    I saw Craig leaning against the counter and he looked up as we came around the corner, "We were beginning to worry about you, slow poke. Well, I guess it's time to get going." He straightened as he held out his hand to Christine. "I need your phone for a second, babe." She handed it over, a rare blush colored her cheeks. Craig tapped on the phone a few times and then his own rang. "Now you've got mine and I've got yours. Use it, yeah?" He handed her back the phone and brushed his lips against her cheek. Oh yeah, I knew she'd be using it.

    They walked past us, headed towards the stairway. Noah's eyes met mine, and I saw confliction in them. I couldn't decipher what he was thinking. As I watched him, I noticed the corners of his gorgeous blue eyes crinkle and he smiled. The conflicted expression was gone, replaced with resolve. Before I could analyze anything, he came up to me with his hand extended. "Your phone, Anna, I need it." Without a thought I pulled it from the tiny bag I held and handed it over to him. He quickly called himself the same way Craig had and handed it back. As my fingers brushed against his, I was hit again with the same electricity I had experienced at the bar. The reaction was thrilling and terrifying at the same time. Though I was still trying to deny it, a small part of me realized something; I liked that sensation.

Noah regarded me, seeing more in my expression than I wanted him to, I'm sure. He placed his hand on my back, low enough that his fingertips grazed my ass, and led me to the stairway. His thumb made small circles against my shirt, rubbing my skin. My skin, and other parts of me, were on fire from the simple, but intimate, gesture. We reached the stairway and Noah leaned in, his warm breath caressed my ears.

"I'm real glad I met you tonight, Anna. I'm looking forward to our date Tuesday night. I normally work late on the last day of demo so I can take my time and make sure everything that needs attention gets it. But knowing I'll see you, well, that's plenty of incentive to cut out early." His words took me by complete surprise. The double meaning dripped from them. I know I had not given any signals that this was a date. Hell, he knew about Roman! Why didn't that drive him off like every other man? I do not have the time or desire to worry about a man, no matter how good it felt when he touched me.

I stared down at my shoes, afraid that if I looked him in the eye I would change my mind, "I had a nice time tonight, Noah, but I'm sorry if you thought Tuesday was a date. I don't do that, date I mean. I don't have time. There's the store, not to mention, Roman? There's too much going on to add a man into my life." Why was I rambling? I don't trip over my words; I make things plain and simple. I make the rules, and rule number one is no dating.

"Anna," My head popped up, and I locked eyes with him, "it's a date. I am attracted to the woman I met tonight. I want to get to know her and see how this goes. We're going to have a good time and eat some first-rate food. You can tell yourself it's not a date all you want, if that makes you feel better, but it's a date. I get where you're coming from, you've got a lot going on, but I'm stubborn when I want something." His words should have upset me. I should tell him to forget about dinner, and Christine and Craig could just go out, but none of that happened. Nope, I just stood there, with my jaw hanging open as he brushed his lips against my cheek and whispered against my skin, "See you soon." I was still standing there, staring at the door a full minute after he was out of sight.

What. The. Hell. How had this happened? I turned from the door and stalked back to the kitchen, angry with myself for being effected by Mr. Caveman. I found Christine sitting at the table, two cups of tea sitting in front of her. She smiled at me for a moment before she let loose. "OK, sis, what do you think? Cute, right? Sweet too. I think this is going to work out perfectly. Dinner will be fun and seeing how he is with Roman will say a lot, don't you think?"

My face heating, and it was not from embarrassment. My anger at myself for my reaction to Noah, now added by my sister's complete disregard for my feelings, was too much.

"I cannot believe you! I have made it clear I don't want to date anyone. I wanted tonight to be about us, hanging out and relaxing. Now I'm stuck having dinner with this guy. I told him no, but did he listen? Of course not. He just told me how it was, and what did I do? Nothing! Not a damn thing, but watch him walk away." My chest heaved with each breath, and I was about to start up again, but Christine beat me to it.

"First of all, missy, I was talking about Craig, remember him? I was thinking seeing how he interacted with my nephew would be a good glimpse at the real him. Not to mention Roman's opinion, kids can read people, you know? But this reaction is way more interesting than my night." She was circling her finger in the air, pointing at me. I realized then that she was enjoying this. "What gives, Anna? You're usually rock solid. Calm and collected in all situations. I cannot even tell you how awesome this is! This guy has you in knots after just a few hours. That alone is worth the rage you just spewed at me." I cocked an eyebrow at her, but she waved me off. "Oh no, this is awesome. He's really affecting you and it's good to see that can still happen." Then her eyes softened, and she all but whispered, "Henry would have wanted this Anna. You know that."

"Don't bring Henry into this. It's not about him. I just don't want to get tangled up with a guy. There is too much in my life for that mess." I sat down, grabbing one of the steaming mugs, and wrapped my hands around it. I bent over, smelling the floral notes of the tea, willing it to clear my mind. I waited for Christine to say more, but nothing came. I snuck a glance up at her and hated what I saw. She was sad; sad for me when she should be happy about the possibilities shown to her tonight. I at once chastised myself for not thinking of her.

"I'm sorry Chris. I had fun tonight even if we had unexpected visitors. I'm glad we had this time out. So, tell me about Craig." That statement seemed to relieve some damage I had done. She smiled at me; a real smile that lit up her eyes, at what I guessed was the thought of Craig. She sang his praises as we finished our tea.

With our cups washed and put away, we said good-night and headed to bed. I stripped off my clothes, tossing them into the wicker hamper and changed into a comfortable pink camisole and pink and white striped cotton pants. I scrubbed my makeup off and stared at myself in the mirror as I applied moisturizer to my face. Tears pricked at the backs of my eyes as I squeezed them shut. I wanted everyone to leave it alone. To leave me alone. I was happy enough. I supported not only myself and Roman, but Christine too. I loved my job, my home, everything. So, why did I suddenly feel like I was missing out on something? My thoughts travelled to Noah and I couldn't help but feel like the fire that trailed across my skin when he touched me was haunting me. I shook my head, ridding myself of the memory.

I lay down in my bed, tossing and turning for what seemed like forever. Looking at the clock I was shocked to see it was nearing one in the morning. I shifted the pillows and tried to find sleep again, but it was no use. Every time I closed my eyes I pictured two of the bluest eyes I had ever seen set on the chiseled face that would not go away. Noah. I swear I could still feel his hand on my back and his lips on my cheek. I started to imagine how it would feel if he had touched me elsewhere, and instead of drifting off to sleep, I succeeded in getting myself flustered and frustrated.

I gave up and reached into the drawer of my nightstand. Just because I didn't have a boyfriend didn't mean I couldn't pretend. I slowly pulled the waist of my pants down, removing them before I came to my senses. I placed the vibrator with practiced precision and let my imagination take over. Noah's hands were my hands, skimming over the tight pebbles on my nipples, massaging my breasts. I imagined his breath against my ear, telling me that he wanted to take care of me. My clit begged for attention and I wasted no time. Rubbing the toy in slow circles, the wave of pleasure was building inside me. I moved my hand, dragging my fingertips across my chest and giving attention to my other nipple, pulling and pinching as I wished Noah had.

As I pushed myself over the edge, I bit down hard on my lip, not letting the moan be released. I sat there for a moment, exhausted from the best orgasm I've had in years. All it took was the right motivation, I guess. I stayed that way for a while, lost in my head. Finally deciding I was able to sleep, I pulled my pants back on. Thoughts of Henry hit me. For the second time that night, I was threatened with tears. What would he want me to do? It had been years since he left us and I had never wanted to talk to him more than I did right now.

Chapter Seven

Noah

I was ripping out the last kitchen cabinets when Craig walked in from the living room. Our first day of demolition proved to be very productive, getting through the entire upstairs. The house was built in the thirties, and it needed more I had originally thought when I bought it, but the deconstruction was going fast. I love a challenge, so this was perfect. When I could take a structure that no one thought to take care of, bring it back to glory, and see a house reach its potential I, well that was its own reward. Making a ton of money on half the sales I got wasn't too bad either.

"I called the trash company and asked if they would add a pickup tomorrow morning. The dumpster got full faster than I expected, but they said it shouldn't be a problem. And, Tony called and said that if he finished up his job earlier than expected, then he could start on our wiring early. Things seem to be falling into place real easy with this one, yeah Noah?" he grabbed pieces of the cabinets and followed me outside to the dumpster.

After throwing them in, I replied, "Yeah, man, everything is coming together better than I planned. The demo will be complete by lunchtime tomorrow. We're making good time on this project." I walked over to my truck, opened the cooler in the bed and pulled out two bottles of water, tossing one to Craig, I added, "We might even have time to shower before dinner with the girls."

He barked out a laugh, "I bet they'd appreciate that." He paused to take a drink before asking me, "So, you and Anna? It's good there? Because I could have sworn I heard her tell you it wasn't a date." His tone was full of humor, but then he added with a more serious tone, "It's ok if you want to back out, yeah? I didn't know she had a kid, you ok with that?" I appreciated, but it was unnecessary. I wasn't worried, and I didn't want him to be.

"It'll be fine, Craig, it's not the same thing. I admit I was on the fence about getting involved with, well, anyone. I hadn't thought I'd want to start anything up with someone with a kid, but there's something that draws me to her, I guess. I'm not going to miss out 'cause that bitch screwed me. You know, Anna told me she doesn't date. Like at all. She's gonna have to get over that shit real quick." I drank half the bottle of water in one gulp, needing the distraction.

Anna had been on my mind since leaving her place Saturday night. Her face kept popping up in my head; her face and her ass. Damn I wanted to follow her up those stairs, hips swinging, every day. I might have started out not wanting a relationship, but when I saw the opportunity to be with someone like Anna, I wasn't fucking around. I understood where she was coming from; you have to be careful when there is a kid involved. I respected the hell out of her for putting him first. I understood it better than she realized.

I took another drink just as my phone rang. When I saw Kiersten's name flash across the screen my heart rate increased. What fucking timing, I wasn't putting up with her shit today. To stay on track, I tossed the now empty bottle in with the rest of the trash and started back into the house. Craig went back to double checking our plans without a word and I went to use my pent-up energy to get the rest of the cabinets outside to be collected by the trash company. I needed to get to pulling up the old linoleum flooring.

***

"Hey Craig?" I hollered out through the window, "Are you ready to get going?" He raised his head from his phone, a toothy grin plastered across his face.

"Yeah man, let's wrap this up. I need to get to the rec center soon. Chris just texted me that the sign-up sheet for Anna's class has been posted. Says it fills up fast and I better hurry. You're still going with me, right? I can't be the only dude in a class of old ladies."

"Well, I don't know, it might be good for you. I don't know if I want to spend what little free time I have on something like that." I had to give him hell, but I had already determined that I'd be at that class. I wouldn't miss an opportunity to get under Anna's skin, knock her off center. No matter what she said, I know what I saw in her eyes. Lust. Desire. Shit like that I can work with. I can just see us in class; I'd need that one-on-one attention with her hands guiding mine. I looked forward to using my hands in other ways with her too. I wanted to grab that perfect heart shaped ass of hers while I pounded into her – "You coming or what?" Craig's voice broke through my thoughts, bringing me back to reality. I took a few awkward steps, my cock straining from my short daydream, grabbed the site plans and jumped into the driver's seat of my truck. We were on our way a minute later, heading to the center. I looked over at Craig, still on his phone, texting Christine I assumed. It had been days, and she had him whipped.

Talking to me without lifting his eyes, he said, "Looks like they want fried chicken tomorrow night. Chris sent me the address so we can swing by anytime we're done, yeah?"

"That sounds good to me. What do you want to do tonight? We can grab a burger and then run over to the realtor's office. When we closed on the house they said they should have listings anytime you want to look." I was sure Craig was even more motivated to find a place of his own, now that he might have someone to come home to. Neither of us had tried very hard since we moved here after we finished the last house. The apartment we were renting was fine for now, but it wasn't home. We both felt like Franklin was a good place to settle down after years of moving from site to site. It had been fun, and we had made a lot of money, but it was time for both of us to put down some roots.

"I called Rich from the realtor's office yesterday actually. He said I could stop by and he would create a list of places for me to check out so that sounds like a plan. Are you still considering staying in the house after we finish it? Or did you have somewhere else in mind?" He raised his eyebrow at me, daring me to deny what we both knew I had been contemplating.

"Nope, I'm thinking living above a pottery store would suit me better," I told him with a laugh. "Now I just have to convince the owner." I hoped that I said the last part to myself, but the laughter coming from the passenger seat told me I had not been quiet enough. I don't know why he was laughing though, I wasn't joking.

Chapter Eight

Anna

By Tuesday I was a mess. I had made it through Monday just fine, with no thoughts of Noah at all. Well, there may have been a couple. I made dinner for everyone; we had watched TV and colored until bedtime, and by then I was so exhausted I was certain I would fall asleep before my head hit the pillow. It wasn't until I finally got to lie down that I found out how wrong I was. I tossed and turned, until I gave in to the fantasy playing in my head, again.

So I woke up this morning tired, and possibly a bit cranky. It didn't help that we had a customer in the store that told me my work resembled amateur, overpriced junk. She said this not only in front of seven other customers here at the time, but Roman heard her and went on a tirade. He yelled at the lady, most of it not able to be understood, until she glared at me and walked out. Roman got so upset I had to carry him up the flight of stairs to his bed where he cried himself to sleep while I held him.

We only had ten minutes left before we closed and I finished ringing up what I hoped would be the last customer when the phone rang, grateful that Christine jumped up and answered it. She came back just as I had flipped over the "open" sign and held the phone out for me. "It's the owner of Rinaldi's, the Italian restaurant we went to with

Mom. They want to talk to you to place an order." I took the phone from her, pointed at Roman behind the counter, and walked into the office.

"This is Anna, what can I do for you?" I had no idea what to expect, at best a special center piece or special planters.

"Anna, my name is Kathryn Rinaldi. I browsed in your store the other day and I noticed your candlesticks. They are exquisite and I would like to place an order for my restaurant. If it's possible, I prefer them to be maroon." Her alto voice carried a faint accent as she spoke.

"Well I don't see a problem with that, Kathryn. Do you have an idea how many pairs you will need and when you'll want them by?" I loved making candlesticks, and now everyone who went to dinner at Rinaldi's would see them. This was amazing.

"Well, I estimate I will need one hundred pairs. There is no hurry; I will replace what I have as you deliver them to the restaurant. My son works in art and I am well aware that no good comes from rushing an artist." My jaw hung open, shocked at the number she ordered. How could a restaurant with twenty-five tables use all of those candlesticks?

"Are you sure you need a hundred?" I sputtered, sure she was mistaken. I didn't want to lose the sale though and immediately regained control on my words. "I would love to make them for you. I am just surprised that you need so many."

Kathryn released a delicate laugh. "Rinaldi's in Franklin is my fourth restaurant. I want all of my tables, at all of my locations, to have them. I hate to even ask, but would it be possible to discuss a price break of sorts, since we are making such a large order with no real deadline?"

We discussed our terms and which styles she preferred of what I had available. The phone call finished up twenty minutes later, and I sat at the desk, still in shock. When it sunk it, I jumped up to tell Christine and Roman the good news. I shoved open the door separating the store from the back of the building while jumping up and down yelling, "One hundred pairs of candlesticks, Chris, can you believe it? And no deadline! Roman! One hundred! It's crazy, they will be in four, yes four, restaurants. Everyone will see them, and they might come here to buy more!" I was still shouting and jumping around when I heard a deep rumble of laugher.

"I'm happy for you, babe. Looks like we got here just in time to celebrate." I froze. It was not Pete's laughter or voice. Shit, I forgot about dinner in my excitement. I turned around to find Craig, Noah, Christine, and Roman smiling at me, trying not to laugh.

The heat of blush tried to creep up my neck, but willed it to stop before I completely embarrassed myself. "Well, I guess you are. Roman, baby, come here and give your Momma a hug. This is a big deal!"

He ran up to me, a wide grin splayed on his face, and I scooped him up. "Is that why you're jumping in the store, Momma? I thought we weren't s'posed to do that?" His eyes were wide, wondering how I could forget.

Properly chastised by a five year old, I dropped my forehead to his. "Momma got excited and forgot, like you do sometimes. I shouldn't jump around in the store either." I tweaked his nose and risked a glance at Noah. He was looking at me. No, not looking, staring, but his eyes were filled with warmth, appreciation, and something else I couldn't quite figure out.

"Well, Rome, how about we get this chicken upstairs and start dinner?" Christine said as she opened the door I had just burst through, Craig trailing behind her carrying our dinner. Noah raised his hand, motioning me to go ahead of him.

I was through the door and almost on the first step when Noah spoke from behind me. "Hey, Roman, if you need a lift, I'll take you. Let's give your Mom a break huh?" His gesture amazed me and I became more stunned when Roman accepted the offer with ease, all but jumping off of me and landing in Noah's arms. I mouthed "Thank you" and started back up the stairs, doing my best not to trip and giving my hips just a touch of extra swing with each step.

Dinner ended up being enjoyable; each of us sharing our day over our favorite fried chicken. I started to get up, reaching for dishes to clear off the table when Noah's large hand covered mine. The touch startled me, causing me to drop my plate. I looked up at Noah, wondering what he was doing. I told him this wasn't a date and Roman was right here, watching. Well, not watching, he was too busy trying to build a larger mashed potato mountain than Christine, but he was right there and isn't blind. I tried to move my hand, but Noah held firm. His callused hands felt rough against mine, but they comforted me at the same time. "Did you n-need s-something?" I breathed, trying for casual, but failing miserably as I stuttered over my words. What was wrong with me?

"Yeah, I need you to leave it for a bit. We'll take care of the dishes later." His authoritative tone should have upset me – commanding me in my home should make me bristle. Instead, I became aroused. My core tightened and my nipples peaked. Apparently not having to do the dishes did it for me. I squirmed in my seat, noticing my sister sneaking glances at me, trying not to laugh at the exchange. I didn't know what to do. It wasn't as if I put myself in these circumstances very often. I decided it wasn't worth arguing over doing the dishes right away. This time. I relaxed back into my seat, forcing a smile at Noah, and pulling my hand back. Noah hesitated for a second, but released me. He nodded at me before his voice quietly rasped out a "Thank you."

Grateful that dinner was over, I ushered Roman to his room to get ready for bed. He had washed up and changed into his pajamas when he asked me for a drink of water. I led him to the kitchen, past the three adults seated on the couches, and filled a small cup for him. When he finished, he ran to his aunt, giving her a big good night hug and kiss. My sister and I exchanged a look when he repeated the gesture with the two men. Roman wasn't this open with new people, and between the ride up the stairs in Noah's arms and the eagerness for hugs, his immediate acceptance of our new friends amazed me.

After I got him to sleep I walked out towards the kitchen, ready to clean up. To my surprise there was nothing left to clean. Even the dry dishes had been put away. I smiled at the group on the couches, "You guys can come over more often if you can get Chris to do the dishes."

"Wasn't me sis. Noah wouldn't let me, said I looked like I needed a break. I refused to take it personally and let him have at it."

I shifted my focus to Noah, who just shrugged his shoulders as if it was no big deal. "I knew you would worry over 'em until they were done, and these two were busy. It's nothing, just being helpful. Tonight has been the most entertaining night we've had since we got here, don't you think Craig?" His eyes never left mine, trying to judge my reaction. The air was thickening with the tension between us, but I refused to give him the satisfaction of showing how flustered I felt. I meant what I told him, this wasn't a date. No matter how much he made it like one.

"Yeah, man, these two ladies are way more fun than you. Prettier too." We all laughed at him as the joke successfully lightened the mood. We talked for a while, laughing at jokes, and learning about each other's lives. It was nice to have them here. The conversation was fun and flowed easily. I was glad I had been roped into dinner tonight. But it still wasn't a date.

When both Christine and I let out a yawn, the guys looked at each other, knowing it was time to call it a night. The disappointment that surged through me to see them leave worried me a little. I should be ready for them to go, not trying to keep them here. Christine walked

Craig the entire way downstairs, but I hated to leave Roman by himself. Noah stopped as he reached the door to the stairwell and grabbed my hand. I steeled myself against the growing desire to lean closer and shift his arm around me. He needed to go before I did something stupid.

"Thanks for having us over tonight. I meant it when I said it was the best night since we got here. The only other that comes close was Saturday." Before I knew what was happening, he leaned in, pulled my hand behind me while pressing it to my back, and kissed me. His lips were soft, and he tasted like beer. I felt him press more firmly into my back as his other hand came behind my head. The intensity of the kiss grew, and I everything else melted away. Just as his tongue swiped across the seam of my lips, asking for entrance, the door swung open and Christine gasped from behind Noah. The spell broke, and I tried to retreat, but he still held my hand firmly in his against my back.

Christine apologized and slid by us before Noah leaned in against my ear, just as he had done the last time we stood here. "G'night darling. I'll call you tomorrow." With that he left. And just like the last time he said goodbye, I was left staring at the door, not knowing how to react.

"Are you going to stare at the door all night or are you going to come in here and explain what I just walked in on?" Christine's shout from the living room pulled me out of my stupor. I turned and walked to the couch. When I sat down, I curled my legs underneath me and hugged one of the pillows. I didn't know what to say. I wavered between showering Noah's scent of off me and reliving the whole scene with my sister. She waited a few heartbeats, letting me settle, before making me spill.

"Alright Banana, I've given you a minute. Now, tell me again how you're not interested in dating Noah? You seemed pretty interested as the two of you were eye fucking all night and I'm pretty sure you're not supposed to suck face with guys you don't want to date." She quirked her lips and held back the laughter I knew was bubbling up inside her.

"There was no eye fucking and what you walked in on was a momentary lapse in judgment. He took me by surprise, is all, and it won't happen again. I don't have time and I won't have a parade of men in and out of Roman's life. This isn't even worth talking about." I was angry now; angry at Noah for kissing me, yes, but more angry that I let him. Hell, I did more than let him. Now I was knocked off kilter, feeling too much about someone I had just met. My world had spun out of control. It was one hell of a kiss though.

"You know sis, it's ok to be a priority too. You are the best mom Roman could ask for. No one is asking you to stop being that for him. We just want you to take care of yourself too. You deserve it, honey. I know you don't want me to say it, but I'm going to anyway. Henry would be so disappointed that you are holding yourself back. He never would have wanted you to be lonely. You have to believe that." Tears filled both of our eyes; I knew she was right.

"I'm so afraid, Chris. So many things could go wrong, and it won't be just me that suffers. I need to think of Roman. Maybe if Noah is willing to go slowly, really slowly, maybe it could work." I stood and walked over to her, giving her a hug. "I need to sleep. It's been a big night." She nodded at me and I turned to go to my room. Shutting the door, I let silent tears stream down my face.

Thinking of Henry was still difficult. We had been friends for so long, I missed having him around every day. I saw him every day in Roman's face, though, and that comforted me. Henry and I didn't have an amazing love story; we weren't in love at all. Oh, we loved each other, but not in the way everyone thought. We got together because we were both lonely, both of us working too much to take the time to meet new people, so we just chose to be together.

Henry was one of the most attractive men in Franklin and I wasn't exactly ugly, so the leap from friends to lovers wasn't too difficult. It certainly helped that it had been a long time since either of us had gotten any. So one night we got drunk, had some fun and the rest was history. A year into the comfortable arrangement, I ended up pregnant with Roman. At first I panicked, but knowing how steady and solid Henry was, it didn't take long for me to become overjoyed. Our relationship strengthened and everyone wondered when we would tie the knot, but we would not get married. I hated to think that Henry would be stuck with me forever if the possibility for him to find real love was out there, and he felt the same way about me. So we would stay like this, and if we met someone, we would figure it out.

We were over the moon in love with our boy though. From the minute Roman was born, Henry wanted to do everything he could to be involved. He moved in here with me to be close. His things were in what was now Christine's room. We still enjoyed the physical aspects of our relationship, when we weren't exhausted, but living together was new, and we both needed our own space. It worked well for our little family; until one day when it was all over. Henry was on his way home from work, when a drunk driver hit his car, killing him instantly. I was devastated for weeks, overwhelmed and alone. I couldn't deal with losing my best friend and Roman's father. Knowing Roman would never meet the amazing person who helped create him was the most heartbreaking part of it all.

After a while, Christine moved in, helping me get through day by day, and eventually it got easier. Roman was a huge part of my recovery. He needed me to keep it together, and I saw so much of Henry in him, so it was like he never really left.

I said a silent prayer for guidance and closed my eyes. I could still see Henry holding his baby boy. Then, as sleep came over me, the picture changed. I saw Roman, as he was now, holding hands with Noah, smiling up at him.

Chapter Nine

Noah

Two weeks. It's been two fucking weeks since we had dinner, and I had not heard much from Anna. I called her, only to go to voicemail. She responded to my texts with simple, one word answers. I understood what she was doing, but I frustrated and everyone around me was paying the price.

I was sitting on the couch in my apartment and staring at the TV while holding a beer when Craig walked into the living room. "What the fuck dude, we gotta go in like 5 minutes or we will be late. Get your ass up and change." He pulled the beer out of my hand and tossed it into the trash. "Where the hell are we going in such a fucking hurry?"

"If you wouldn't have spent the last couple of weeks pouting, you might have remembered we have a class tonight." He gave me a pointed look, holding my eye a minute before it hit me.

"Shit, tonight is Anna's pottery class. Damn it, why didn't you say something. Fuck changing, let's just go." I grabbed my wallet and keys from the table by the door and walked out to my truck. I glanced across the cab to find Craig laughing at me as he got in.

"Thanks for the ride, brother. Glad you decided to tag along." He kept laughing as I peeled out of the parking lot. I didn't care though; I was on my way to see my girl. She didn't know it yet, but she was mine and I would not let her slip through my fingers.

When we found the right room, I saw that Craig had been correct; the room was filled with sweet little old ladies. I scanned the space Anna, but I couldn't find her. I was about to walk out to search of her when two little arms wrapped around my leg. I lowered my eyes to find Roman smiling up at me. "Hey Noah! You here to learn to throw?" He seemed to be happy I was there, and that made my chest tighten. "Well, I don't think your mom wants me to throw anything, do you?" I placed my hand on his head and ruffled his hair.

"Throwing clay is exactly what I want you to do." That sexy voice that came from behind me was unmistakable and I turned to find Anna. I couldn't help but smile as I placed my hand on her hip. Her eyes went down to focus on my hand for a split second, and then back up at me before continuing, "That's what it's called, throwing clay. Why don't you find a seat and we'll start class in a minute."

She tried to move out of my grip, but I pressed my fingers a bit more firmly into her flesh. I looked right into her chocolate eyes and saw the same desire that was there two weeks ago, but there was something else and; a hint of fear. Was she afraid of me? I didn't think that kiss was out of line enough to make her scared of me so that couldn't be it. It must be the audience we had. I released her, not wanting to make her uncomfortable. She brushed past me, close enough that her scent filled me... peaches. Damn, that was sexy.

The class was genuinely fun and the bowl I made didn't even look like shit when we everything was said and done. Anna gave everyone the attention they needed, even helping me by placing her hands over mine to show me the right pressure. I might have messed up a few times on purpose, and I thought I was pretty slick about it until one of the old ladies called me out, but it was worth it to see the blush across Anna's face.

She and Roman were cleaning up one of the older women's stations when I came up behind her. "Think I can get a private lesson some time?" I waggled my eyebrows at her when she spun around and rewarded me with a laugh. She caught her breath, and her sassy mouth deflected the innuendo, "No way, Romeo. This is not Ghost, and you are definitely not Patrick Swayze."

One of the ladies from class shouted from across the room, "Honey, if she won't give it to you, I will!" Anna blushed as I turned and winked. I don't even know if I winked at the right person, but everyone laughed at that; even Anna. I hoped I was getting through that thick head of hers.

With everyone but the three of us gone, I helped Anna pack up what supplies she had left and take them over to her Jeep. I could tell that she was thrown when I offered to help because she just stood there for a second before pointing to a box. I knew then she had been on her own for way too damn long. She didn't think to let people, other than family, help and I wasn't even sure how much she let them help her either.

I loaded the last box when Roman came up beside me. "Um, Noah, you wanna come watch a movie? Momma said I got to if I was good for the whole class." How the hell do I say no to that? Not that I really wanted to. I looked up at Anna to see her mouth formed into a little "O" trying to figure out how to get out of the offer. I ran with it before she could get a word out. "If it's okay with your mom, Roman, I'll even pick up pizza on the way." If looks could kill, I'd be a dead man. Razor sharp daggers shot out of Anna's eyes until Roman turned to her, "Please Momma? We won't even wrestle, I swear." Hopeful eyes and a well-practiced quivering chin won her over. Her eyes bounced from Roman back to me, knowing she was defeated.

"OK, fine, but we better hurry. Bedtime still stands and if the movie isn't over, it's too bad." She walked over to the driver's door, which I opened for her, and got in. Before I shut the door, I leaned in and gave her a quick kiss on the cheek. I heard her gasp in a breath, surprised that I did it front of Roman, and shut the door.

We were at the table, finishing up our pizza, when the family drama started. I just sat back and watched the fireworks.

"Momma, I need a football." That got a glance. "Momma, when I get my football, you gotta show me how to throw it. You're gonna right?" Anna almost choked on her pizza then. They started going back and forth about when they might be able to find time, and maybe Pete could help (who the hell is Pete?), and on and on and on until I finally decided to be the hero.

"Bud, I'll tell you what, if your mom's friend Pete can't find the time to teach you, I will." I bit out the word friend, irritated at the possibility of competition.

"Brother."

What? "What?"

"Peter, he's my brother. I'm sure he can find time on the weekend to help Rome out. Right baby? He said he would." She smiled at both of us, pleased with her solution; one that didn't include me I noticed. But hell, at least I didn't need to stress over Pete..

"Hey, don't worry about that." I smiled at both of them. "I have time in the evenings, and it's still staying light past quitting time. I'll come by a couple of times a week and take Roman over to the park. We'll hang out and play some football and you can feed me dinner. Then when the weekend comes we can show Uncle Pete what he's learned. See? Works out great." I leaned back, clasping my hands behind my head, proud of myself. Then I looked at Anna and I swear my balls shrank. She was pissed, and hell if I knew why.

"That's really nice of you, Noah." She turned to Roman and smiled. Or at least I think it was supposed to be a smile, but it was scary. Shit, I'm in trouble. "Roman, honey, why don't you go wash up and change your clothes while Noah and I clean up dinner." He shifted his eyes back and forth between Anna and me and bolted without a backwards glance; smart kid.

Once he was gone, I stuck a toe into the raging river that was Anna. "Babe, I see that you're mad and I'm thinking it's about something I said. If Pete wants to teach him football that bad, then fine, I'll step back. But you have got to talk to me."

"This doesn't have anything to do with Pete, Noah. You should not make promises to my son without talking to me first. If I say no, then I'm the bad guy and you're the hero. What are you doing with him, huh? You think you'll get to me through Roman? Butter him up to play it against me? That's a crap thing to do and you know it." She was breathing heavy and ready for more. But now I was mad too.

"Are you fucking serious? Using him?! That's what you think? I was trying to be nice. It didn't look like you were jumping at the chance to take him out and toss the ball around. I don't have shit to do but work, so excuse the fuck out of me for wanting to fill my time with some fun."

I don't know when I moved, but now I was inches from her face. We stood there, glaring at each other, until Roman bounded back in, movie in hand. Anna broke eye contact first and went to start the movie while I started throwing away the trash from dinner.

When I lifted my head, I saw them on the couch. Roman cuddled up lying on Anna's chest with her arms wrapped around him. I was shaken by that image. My chest ached, and I at once understood why Anna had jumped me; she was protecting Roman. He had been left before by his dad, and she didn't want that for him again. In that instant

I saw the life I wanted – to be their protector, their refuge from pain and disappointment. The anger that had been coursing through me vanished. How could I be upset with her for doing what was natural. I moved to the couch, picking up Anna's feet and placing them on my lap. She resisted at first, but let out a soft moan of relaxation when I began to massage the arch of her foot. I felt the tension in her body melt away and knew that my message was understood. I was sorry, but I wasn't going anywhere.

Chapter Ten

Anna

As the weight pressing down on me decreased, I wrapped my arms tighter, not wanting to let go. "Anna," a familiar voice whispered, "babe, let him go." I woke up gradually, blinking my eyes while they took in my surroundings. Why was I on the couch? I saw Roman sleeping on my chest and it came back to me. Blinking my eyes, trying to focus, I realized that the TV was off; we had fallen asleep during the movie. I looked up to see Noah with his hands under Roman; he must have been trying to pick him up while I was sleeping.

"Anna," I looked at him, warmed to the core by the emotion in his eyes. "Let me put him to bed. You gotta let go babe, unless you want me to carry both of you," he finished with a smirk and his eyes crinkled in humor. I silently released Roman so Noah could carry him to his room, and I swear I saw him bend to kiss him on the forehead as he walked away.

While Noah was gone, I decided to pick up the living room, but noticed that Noah had beaten me to it. It was then that I realized I was in serious trouble. How in the hell was I supposed to steel myself against falling for this man when he kept surprising me with his thoughtfulness? For a bossy guy that doesn't seem to take no for an answer, he took care of me as if he had been doing it his whole life; as if

I *was* his whole life. This was moving so fast, it had only been a few weeks since we met, but when Noah and I were together, and especially when Roman was with us, it just felt, well, right.

The sound of footsteps made me look up, and spotting Noah, I couldn't help but smile. He smiled back at me as if he knew what I had just admitted to myself. I watched as he moved across the room to sit next to me. We were quiet for a few minutes, gathering our thoughts. I didn't know what he was going to say, but I knew it was going to be important; this was a turning point. Do I go back, or do I take that leap forward?

Noah cleared his throat, bringing me out of my thoughts. "I get it, babe." The way his lips tipped up showed me that my confusion was written all over my face. "I get why you reacted that way. You were protecting him. But you need to know, you don't have to do that. I'm not going to hurt Roman. I will not hurt either of you, and it's time for you to accept that. We have a shot at something good, something solid. But if you don't want it, tell me now, before it goes too far. I don't want to, but if you can't do this, I'll walk away. For you, and for Roman."

His eyes bore into mine, searching for an answer. All I could do was stare back at him. My insides churned with conflict and questions. Was I ready for this? Was Roman? "What ifs" ran through my head with so much force I became dizzy. I sucked in a deep breath and all I heard was my heart pounding in my ears. Noah took my hand, and I at once calmed down. The real question was: could I really let him go? I leaned over, taking his rugged face in my hands, and pressed a gentle kiss to his lips.

Noah didn't respond for a second, and I assumed that he was afraid it was a kiss goodbye. But when I didn't back away, his hands moved to hold me to him, one going to the back of my head and the other wrapped around my waist. He deepened the kiss, making me gasp. He took the opportunity to slide his tongue into my mouth, gently massaging mine. Our tongues danced back and forth, plundering from each other. He leaned into me, pushing me back on to the couch until I was pinned under his weight, our lips never separating.

My senses were overwhelmed. Noah's large arousal pressed against my thigh, the dampness gathering between my thighs, the softness of his lips mixed with the urgency of the kiss. I could taste him, salty and buttery from the popcorn. Noah's pine scent filled me. His hand slowly glided to the hem of my shirt, his fingers brushing my skin. They travelled with intent up my side until he reached my aching breasts. His thumb caressed the tight peak of my nipple through the lace of my bra and I couldn't hold back the moan. My response was rewarded with a deep growl from the back of Noah's throat.

Suddenly Noah pulled back, just enough to look me in the eye. "We gotta stop, babe. There is nothing more I want than to fuck you right here, right now, but our first time together isn't going to be like this. I'm going to get you alone and in my bed. It won't be right after a fight, either. I can't give that to you tonight. But it's gonna happen soon, got me?"

Oh, I got him. Roman was just on the other side of the door and Christine could walk in any second. I cannot believe I let it get this far. I nodded at him, and his lips met mine is a sweet, chaste kiss.

Noah lifted himself up and then held out a hand, pulling me to my feet. His arm snaked back around my waist as he bent, kissing my forehead. He straightened, and then asked, "Who's the guy on Roman's nightstand?" I stiffened, knowing the picture he was referring to. My throat tightened, tears pricked at the backs of my eyes. I had to clear my throat before answering.

"That's Roman's father, Henry." That was all I could say without breaking down. As soon as I thought of Henry I felt guilty. It was irrational and misplaced, but it wasn't as if Henry hadn't wanted to be here. He loved Roman more than life, and in his way, he loved me too. I'm not sure exactly what Noah saw on my face, but his showed a mix of anger and hurt. Unsure of how to handle the conversation I rose onto my toes and kissed his cheek.

"It's late and we both have to work tomorrow. You'll call?" I couldn't hide the insecurity in my voice. Noah cupped the side of my face, searching my eyes before he pressed his forehead against mine. "Yeah babe, I'm gonna call. Get some rest." He turned towards the stairwell door, stopping just a few inches from it. "Tomorrow ok for me to take Roman to the park? I'm just going to be getting deliveries, so I won't be getting a lot done on the site. I could swing by around four and have him home by five."

I knew he was asking about more than football, so I responded the only way I could, "What do you want for dinner?" The dazzling smile Noah gave me blew me away, forcing me to give him one in return. "Whatever you want, babe, whatever you want." With that he opened the door and started down the stairs. I moved the few feet to my room and got ready for bed. When I finally got to lie down, I drifted off to sleep, smile still firmly in place.

Chapter Eleven

Noah

Craig and I were helping unload the last delivery of the day at three thirty. The truck had been late, and I was livid. Craig and the men from the lumber yard were doing their best to keep up with me, but none of them had the motivation I did.

The driver said there a flat tire caused the delay or some bullshit. To be honest, I wasn't really listening to excuses by the time he arrived. I just got to work unloading the truck so I could get the hell out of here. I could not believe that my first attempt to show Anna that I would not let her or Roman down got so fucked up. I couldn't allow myself be too late; I was hauling ass to finish. Craig was pacing himself right along with me, knowing I wanted to get done. He hadn't asked about my plans, but I was sure Christine had told him.

It was five minutes before four when we finally got everything unloaded. There was no way I would be on time, so I shot a quick message to Anna telling her I'd be there in fifteen minutes. I had gone less than a mile when my phone alerted me to a new text message. I checked it at the first stop I came to and panicked. All it said was "Hurry" with no explanation.

I slammed the truck in park in front of the store fifteen minutes later, leaping out and running to the door, ripping it open. There were only a couple of people in the store besides Anna, but everyone jumped a little when I burst in. "What happened?" I asked, half out of breath from fear. Roman's little arms wrapped around my leg tightly and I looked down to see an enormous smile across his face. I was really confused now.

Anna appeared baffled for a second, and then took a deep breath, "I'm sorry Noah, I wasn't thinking, nothing happened."

"You told me to hurry. What's going on?"

"I know and I'm sorry. I was busy when I got your message. Nothing is wrong, it's just…" She broke off, and shifted her eyes to Roman, who was still hugging my leg. "He has been at the window for the last hour constantly asking if you might get here early. I'm sorry Noah; I was getting frustrated with customers and the phone ringing. I didn't think about how it could sound."

Her handsome face was so apologetic; I couldn't help but grin at her. "It's fine. I was worried, but it's fine. I'm sorry I was running behind." I looked down at Roman and ruffled his hair. "Ready to go bud?" He nodded once before flying out of the store and jumping into the truck.

"I guess he's excited, babe. So, what's for dinner?" The corners of her mouth tipped up, holding back a laugh. "We're having tacos, but it won't be ready until after six, so there's no rush." I reached out, wrapping my fingers around the curve of her hip, and pulled her against me. Her body melted into me as I brushed my lips against hers.

"We'll be back after a while." I moved away, causing her to stumble a little when I released my grip. Roman had his nose pressed to the window and the football in his hand, waving for me to hurry when I got outside. I opened the door and offered him my hand, "Rome, buddy, it's like 4 blocks to the park. We're walkin' there."

Roman and I were about three feet apart and had been tossing the ball and goofing off for approximately twenty minutes when the picture on his nightstand popped in my mind. I really wondered how a dad could leave his kid, especially Roman. After a few more minutes I got the balls to ask the question that had been running through my mind.

"Hey, bud?" he looked at me, eyes shining, "does your dad ever bring you to the park?" As the question came out, he faltered a moment, dropping the ball. Picking it up, he glanced up at me, and I knew the answer. Well, I thought I did, and I was angry. But I was not ready for what Roman said next.

"No. My dad died. I was still a baby, so I don't really remember him. But, Momma says he woulda brung me." He shrugged his shoulders and then tossed me the ball.

I was floored. I had assumed that Anna worried I would just ditch her one day like her ex, but she never even hinted that Roman's father had died. Shit, they would still be together today. I would not have even had a chance. I wasn't sure how to handle the mix of emotions coursing through me. Yes, I was upset that Anna and Roman were made to deal with that sort of loss, but I was also grateful for the opportunity to have a place in their lives, and that made me feel like an asshole.

We tossed the ball awhile longer until Roman got bored and ran over to the slides. At five-thirty I propped him up on my shoulders and walked back to the store. We both gave Christine a wave as we walked through and I carried Roman up the stairs where we found Anna. Roman went to wash up, and I went to see if I could help.

Walking up behind her, I placed my hands over her hips, pressing a kiss to her neck. We stood that way for a few minutes until I got my shit together enough to talk to her. "Had an interesting conversation with Roman at the park. Why didn't you tell me about Henry? I thought he left you guys." I tried not to make it sound like an accusation, but by the way she stiffened, I'm pretty sure I failed.

Without me letting her go, Anna turned around to face me. She took a deep breath, and her whole body shivered as it pressed against me. "It's hard to talk about. I never told you he left us, but I realize it's a natural assumption, and I am sorry I let you think it." Anna took a deep breath before continuing. "Henry died when Roman was still a baby. A drunk driver hit him. I didn't know how to bring it up to you. Everyone I know already knows what happened, so it has not been an issue before." She sniffed, and I kicked myself for not being gentler with her.

Her breathing was becoming ragged, and I wasn't sure if it was from thinking about Henry or if she was afraid of my reaction. I pulled her close and stood there for a minute with my chin resting on the top of her head. Taking some deep breaths, I took my time figuring out what to say.

"Anna, I'm sorry." She jerked back, surprised by my words. "Babe, I thought I was chasing away bad memories of some jerk who ditched you when you needed him. I didn't even consider you might have still wanted Roman's dad in your life. It's been a long time though. So, I have to ask, are you ready for this?"

I cleared my throat, afraid of what she would say; God I hope she says yes. I don't think I can handle anything else. She looked down at the floor, and my gut clenched.

Her eyes lifted, uncertainty obvious, "Noah, I'm ready to try, that's all I can promise. Is that enough?"

I cupped her chin with my hand and kissed her hard. "It's more than enough, babe. More than enough."

Chapter Twelve

Anna

I was in the studio, mixing clay bricks in my pug mill, when the lamp flickered and Christine walked in, fuming. "I don't know what the hell is wrong with that man! How can he say that I'm taking sides? And even if it was, of course I would take your side."

What the hell was she talking about? I tried to ask, but she just kept yelling, "So what if Noah didn't have all the details about Henry, it's not like you guys have been together for years while you kept some deep dark secret. What. The. Fuck." She punctuated the last three words by jabbing her finger into the air in front of me. She was sucking in breath after breath, trying to calm herself. I would have tried to help, but I was too confused.

"Chris, what are you saying? Why do you need to take my side? Craig, and I'm just guessing that's who this rant is over, doesn't know what he's talking about. Noah didn't leave upset. At least, I didn't think he did."

I replayed the other night in my head, still rather sure of my answer. Noah said trying was enough, and I apologized for not explaining what really happened to Henry. We were fine, right? What if we weren't? We hadn't spoken in a few days, just a few short texts.

Maybe he got mad after thinking it over. Well, if he's mad and not talking to me to clear things up, then why

My heart pounded in my ears; it pissed me off that he would complain to someone else and not me, "You know what, Chris? This is exactly why I didn't want to date in the first place. Well, he can just be mad. It's not like he actually asked me to explain what happened with Henry. Argh." I finished packaging the clay bricks and started cleaning. I looked over at Christine and saw guilt etched on her face. "You know what, Banana? Maybe Craig got it wrong. Let's not jump to conclusions about Noah. I... I just," she paused, and her hesitation just made me even more upset.

"Spit it out Chris, what?" I snapped at her.

"It's just that... shit Banana, Noah is the first guy in years you've been interested in. I don't want you to throw that away when we don't know what happened. All Craig said to me was that it wasn't fair of you to lie about Henry. I, of course, told him that it wasn't a lie, and then we started arguing over what counts as a lie, and I hung up on him and he hasn't called since."

The words flew out of her mouth at lightning speed right before she burst into tears, collapsing on a nearby chair. It wasn't often my sister's emotions got the best of her, so seeing her like this shocked me. I had been so caught up in my own new man; I hadn't even thought to talk to her about her own.

I washed my hands without hesitation and put my arms around her. She settled down after a few minutes, when she asked, "What time is Roman going to be back from Mom's? Do we have time for a beer?" Her eyes said it all, she needed me right now.

"Let me text Mom and ask her to keep him longer. We'll go get a beer."

***

We had just settled into a corner booth at Fritz's when Christine's phone chimed. She looked at it, but set it back down on the table with no response. I studied her as she fingered the peeling label of her bottle. She was upset in a way I hadn't seen before. Christine hadn't told me what was said during their argument, but it must have been harsh. Her phone went off two more times without her checking it before I finally get the nerve to ask, "Are you going to even see what it says?"

"Nope. I need time." She lifted her bottle to her lips, taking a long pull.

"So, c'mon, what happened?"

"I told you what happened. We don't agree on what parts of our past, anyone's really, are lies by omission. I think there are some things, personal things, that you don't have to tell anyone unless you want to. Craig didn't understand why, and he then demanded to know what I wasn't telling him. Then it became a trust issue, and I hung up on him. Now he thinks there's some dark scary secret and he won't let it go." She sighed, grabbing her phone as she gave in to the temptation.

We finished our beers with little conversation. I had to wonder if there was something Christine wasn't telling Craig. When I couldn't think of anything she would hide, I wondered if she had kept something from me. I forced the idea away; these guys would not make me question my own sister. No way.

After we picked Roman up from our parent's house, the three of us drove home in silence. I wondered why Roman hadn't been talkative, but I just assumed he was tired. Pulling into the driveway, I glanced back and saw Roman had fallen asleep. I motioned to Christine, and she helped me with the doors so I could carry him up the stairs.

I was a few steps behind her when she let out a short gasp of surprise, so I hurried my steps to find both Craig and Noah waiting on the steps to the back door. Without a sound, Noah came over and lifted Roman into his arms. His tee shirt showed the flex in his arms as he held my son, and the vision had warmth spreading throughout me.

Upon entering the apartment, Noah and I went to Roman's room and settled him in bed. I gave him a quick kiss on the forehead before walking out. Noah wrapped an arm around my shoulders and my traitorous body melted right into him. I was still upset he had thought I lied to him; I shouldn't be putty in his arms.

Instead of going into the living room, Noah steered me towards my bedroom. I stiffened slightly; no man had been in there other than Henry. As if he sensed my hesitation, Noah leaned over and pressed his lips to my ear. "I just want to give them some time alone. I don't expect anything right now. Besides, babe, we need to talk. Craig told me about his fight with Chris after I jumped his ass about his attitude today. Since we only take one vehicle to the site most days, I just drove him here. This way I can make sure you and I are okay while they work out their issues." I nodded at him and went through the doorway.

I sat on the edge of my bed and braced for whatever Noah would say. "Okay, Noah, what's up?" I tried, and failed, for chipper. He tipped his head to one side, his lips turning up at the corners. I watched as he walked over, stopping next to me and sat down. Rolling his shoulders as if stressed, his voice was low and gravelly.

"I'm not mad, Anna, never was. When Craig got around to telling me what crawled up his ass, the first thing I wanted to do was make sure that you didn't think I felt the same way. I'm already fighting a ghost. I don't want to have to fight other people's bullshit too."

My eyes stayed trained on the wall in front of me, his eyes boring into me as he spoke. I let his words sink in before turning and taking in his face. I could stare at him for hours. His blonde hair had grown out a bit since we met; it hung just above his eyes now. And those eyes, they were oceans of blue that expressed so many emotions I couldn't look away if I wanted to. I grabbed his hand, loving how mine fit inside his; like they were made for each other.

We sat there in silence for a few minutes; just enjoying being together, waiting for the storm in the living room to pass. Noah placed his other hand on my back, making slow, gentle circles.

At first the touch calmed me, offering me the sensation of being safe and taken care of, but when his hand slipped under the hem of my shirt, the gentle caress pushed my body into overdrive. I laced our fingers together, my grip strengthening, and the minutes ticked by. The tension built throughout my body until I could no longer ignore it.

A moan escaped my lips as the pressure from Noah's fingers grew. I twisted to face him and placed my free hand on his jaw. I moved closer, intending to give him a reassuring kiss, when Noah's arm wrapped around me and he flipped his body over mine and laid me back as if I weighed nothing.

As my head hit the pillow, Noah's lips crashed into mine. The heat of desire seared our kiss as our hands moved in wild abandon, tugging at our clothes. My shirt was yanked over my head and thrown away. I decided it was only fair to strip him so I reached for his shirt, but Noah wasn't waiting for me. He grabbed the back of his shirt, pulling it over his head. I drank in the site of his toned body, sprinkled with hair that left a trail all the way down past the waist of his jeans.

He stared at me as I was displayed on the bed. The I squirmed under the intensity of his gaze.. "Anna, you are the most stunning woman I have ever laid eyes on. I have been dreaming about this for weeks. Let me see you." The need in his voice calmed me and I stopped shifting. The look of pure appreciation on Noah's face as his eyes raked my body made me feel sexier than I had in a long time – maybe ever.

Noah lowered himself back onto me, holding his weight up with his forearms. He trailed kisses from my jaw line down my neck, pausing above the lace of my bra. I arched my back, my body begging him to continue. With a quick tug, my breast was exposed, the heat from his breath on my nipple, sending ripples of pleasure the length of my body.

As he took the tight bud into his mouth, dampness pooling between my thighs. A quick nip of his teeth had me biting back a moan. Noah's fingers traced random patterns on my stomach, inching lower with every stroke.

The murmur of voices broke my concentration. My mind was racing with thoughts of Roman, Christine, and Craig being right on the other side of the door. As if he could read my thoughts, Noah brought his face to mine and whispered against my lips, "Anna, it's just us, please don't make me stop."

Make him stop? How could I do that? My whole body was on fire and Noah was the only thing that could dampen the flames. I responded to his plea by unbuttoning his jeans and putting my hands beneath them. My hands landed on his perfect ass and I couldn't help but squeeze the firm muscle. Another growl came from his throat as he nipped at my other breast. His once tender fingers plunged desperately into my pants, tugging at them. As I tipped my hips to help remove the boundary between us, Noah moved down my body and pulled the fabric as he went, trailing kisses the whole way.

As my pants hit the floor, Noah slipped my legs over his shoulders. He licked a path from my knee to the center of my thighs. He kissed me over the thin cotton of my panties and inhaled deeply. "God babe, you smell so fuckin' sweet. I can't wait to taste you. I bet it's better than honey." With that, he seized the thin strip of fabric ripping it clean off and stared right at me.

The lust that clouded his eyes more than made up for the apprehension I felt being on total display. He kissed me again and let his tongue glide up my slit coming just short of my clit, teasing me.

He began switching back and forth from licking to sucking in a steady, mind numbing rhythm,, driving me crazy. My hands threaded through his hair, gripping lightly. He growled at the touch and intensified his effort. My orgasm began building as I writhed beneath him. As he gripped my hips harder, pinning me in place, Noah drove his tongue into me, forcing a moan out of me.

The reaction spurred him on, and as he sucked my clit into his mouth, he plunged two fingers into my soaked channel, pushing me over the edge. My hips bucked, and I grabbed a handful of Noah's hair as my body was overtaken with wave after wave of pleasure.

My legs slipped from his shoulders as he stood. I saw he still had his pants on so I reached for them, needing him inside me now.

As if he read my thoughts, he lowered himself over me once again. My hands went to his back, nails scratching his skin as I pulled him closer. He settled between my legs, his thick arousal pressed against my belly. As my hand reached him, there was a knock on my door. Noah cursed under his breath before answering with a curt, "What?"

Craig's voice came through, "Hey man, you ready to go?" Noah thrust a hand into his hair. He looked into my eyes, mirroring my frustration. I wanted him to tell Craig to take the truck and pick him up in the morning, but I wasn't ready for the questions that a sleepover would cause. Noah watched me, opened his mouth to say something, but quickly shut it. With a shake of his head, he leaned down and kissed me with tenderness, giving me a hint of my own flavor.

He turned his head towards the door and shouted, "Give me a minute, man." Pulling me to my feet, Noah wrapped an arm around my middle, closing the gap between us. "Babe, he's gotta go. I can hear it in his voice. I hadn't planned on us getting to this point tonight and I don't want to stop here, but I know you're not comfortable with me staying the night. I need to go with him." He dipped his head and ran his nose along my law line, kissed me gently on the lips, and skimmed his mouth up to my ear where he whispered, "Like fuckin' candy, Anna. You taste like fuckin' candy. It's mine now, you got that?"

Oh, yeah, I got that. I couldn't make myself say it out loud though, so I just nodded. Noah needed to leave, so I picked up my shirt and pulled it on while searching for my pants. Noah and I finished dressing in silence, the intensity of what we had shared hung in the air.

He opened the door to leave, but turned, pulling me to him. "Thank you for that, babe. Thank you for trusting me to be in here," he said as he pointed around my room before touching his finger to my chest, right over my heart. "I'm gonna work damn hard to get in there too."

He didn't realize how close he already was. It hadn't been very long, and we barely knew each other, but Noah made me feel things I never have before. It was definitely too soon to tell him, too soon to be sure and solid, but Noah Evans had already worked his way into my heart.

There were so many emotions running through me, I thought I was going to faint. Instead, I just pushed up on my toes and brushed my lips against his. Grabbing his hand, he led me out the door to the stairway.

"I'll call you tomorrow, okay babe?"

"Yeah, that sounds good, Noah."

With one last quick kiss goodbye, Noah followed Craig down the stairs. I shut the door behind them and turned to search out my sister. As much as I was dealing with, judging by Craig's need for a fast escape, I knew she needed me right now.

I found her curled up on the couch nursing a bottle of beer. She looked tired and defeated. I wasn't sure what to say to her right away, so I veered to the kitchen for my own bottle. I twisted the cap off and tossed it into the trash can slowly, stalling for time. I needed to move past what had happened with Noah in my bedroom before I went to my sister.

Giving my head a quick shake and rolling my shoulders, I made my way to the other couch. I sat there watching Christine for a few minutes. She was devastated and trying not to show it.

"So, what happened with Craig tonight?"

"I'm not sure. He says I made it sound like I had secrets I was keeping from him. I just don't think that everything that has happened in my life is up for grabs, you know?"

I nodded, but the impression she was keeping something from me crept back in. I think I knew how Craig was feeling, I didn't care for it and I understood why he didn't either.

"Well, sometimes something that we think is small means a lot to someone else. Is there something that you don't think is important? Maybe he's reading more into it than he should. But if there is something, well then he isn't wrong."

"Oh, not you too! Look, I'm going to bed. I've had enough of this shit tonight. Leave me alone." Christine got up and stalked to her room, taking her beer. The door slammed behind her, making me jump. Now I knew Craig was right. But Christine wasn't just keeping something from him. She was keeping it from all of us.

Chapter Thirteen

Noah

As much as I wanted to kill Craig for interrupting me and Anna, it was probably for the best. I had not planned for us to get that hot and heavy tonight, but I couldn't regret it. Damn, she was perfect. I don't know what happened to my self-control, but something just clicked when I heard that low, sexy moan come from her.

I had planned on talking to her and going slow, but with her as into it as I was I couldn't stop myself. No freaking way. I saw her disappointment when we had to stop, but she was relieved as well. I could tell she what was happening between us scared her. I just had to prove to her that this thing between us was real.

Driving us back to the apartment, the anger pulsed out of my friend. He clenched and relaxed his hands, wanting to hit something. When we reached the apartment I grabbed two beers and handed him one. He took it without a word and sat on the couch.

I stayed in the kitchen, leaning against the counter knowing that if he wanted to talk he would. I pulled out my phone and sent a quick text.

Me: Night babe

Anna: You too

Anna: Thanks

I snorted at that. She was going to have to be more specific.

Me: For what?

Anna: For making sure we were okay

Not what I expected. My chest clenched at the idea of us not being ok.

Me: Always

I waited a few minutes, but there was no response. I looked up at Craig. He was angry, yeah, but more, he was hurt. I don't know what happened, but we weren't big on heart to hearts, so I wasn't going to press him. It'll come out at some point; if she means that much he'll want advice soon enough.

"Hey man, I'm gonna get some sleep. We'll start at 7, yeah?"

"Fine."

Well, okay then. I made my way to my room. I stripped off my shirt, imagining how Anna's fingernails had felt as she drew them across my back. My dick twitched at the memory. We were going to have to get some alone time soon.

I grabbed my phone on the way to the shower. I had a couple pictures of Anna and I was going to need them tonight.

I soaped my body and fisted my cock, imagining my hand was Anna's. I glanced through the glass door at my phone I had propped up on the counter. God, she was gorgeous. I was rock hard, remembering the taste of her sweet pussy on my tongue, and the sound of Anna's moans as she clenched around my fingers. When she came it was music to my ears.

My hand moved faster, I was so close. I wondered how damn good it would be to have her lips wrapped around my cock instead of my hand. I could almost see it. My fingers threaded through her dark hair, guiding her back and forth, while I fucked her mouth. It was too much. I went off like a rocket, spraying cum on the wall.

The release had barely made a dent in my need to be in her, I was going to have to get her under me again. She was so far under my skin I could barely see straight. I have never felt like this about a woman. Even Kiersten hadn't meant this much; not that *she* ever really meant a lot, only what I thought she was giving me did.

I turned the water off, rubbing my hair with a towel, trying to rid myself of thoughts of her. The thought of Kiersten turned my stomach now. There was a time I thought she would be in my life forever. I'm just glad I didn't let her shit screw up my time with Anna.

I dropped down on the bed. Exhausted from the day, I was asleep in no time.

***

The next morning was warm. It was tough to work in because of the heat and humidity. My tee shirt already clung to my skin, and we had been working for a just couple hours.

The heat hadn't improved Craig's mood any either. He was stomping around, pissed at everyone. I was going to ask him what crawled up his ass when my phone went off.

Anna: Are you going to take Roman to the park today?

It had been a few days since our last "practice session." I wanted to go, but the heat was going to make getting through the day hard.

Me: Not sure depends on how the day goes

Anna: k

If one word answers were bad, one letter can't be good at all. I knew Roman was expecting me. Hell, he wanted me to come every day. Don't get me wrong, I wanted to be there, but we had deadlines on this house.

Letting out a big sigh, I did the only thing I could do.

Me: I'll be there after 6. What's for dinner?

Anna: Whatever you want

Me: Careful babe I might get ideas

Anna: ;)

A damn wink in a text had my dick twitching. Hell, let's be honest – I didn't even need that. I sat there for a minute, smiling like an idiot at my phone.

"What the hell are you smiling about? Get your ass back to work!"

I looked up to see Craig making his way toward me. "You know what, Craig. You've been storming around with a stick up your ass. Call her and get over yourself. Don't be mad because I got my girl making me dinner."

"Fuck you, man. You don't know shit." Craig's whole body changed. His face turned red, his shoulders drooped, and his fists balled at his sides. His feelings for Christine ran much deeper than I thought.

"Hey, you want to talk to her, then go talk to her. Don't give her the option of not picking up by calling. Go to her. The two of you seemed to start off pretty strong. What the hell happened?"

"I don't know!" He screamed as his face turned beet red. Then he whispered like he was in pain, "I don't know. I was mad that you did not know the truth about Roman's dad and said some shit about lies of omission. Then all of a sudden, Christine got really defensive and said not everything in life is up for discussion. Made me wonder, you know?"

I understood what he was saying. I would probably think she was keeping something from me too. "Yeah, I get you. What did you do?"

"I yelled at her. I asked her if she was keeping anything from me. She asked if I was calling her a liar and we just started screaming at each other." He hung his head as if defeated. "That's when she hung up on me. I went to her last night to try to work it out, but something was off. I don't know what's going through her head, but man, the way she reacted, I know there's something she isn't telling me."

Craig had been through his own tough relationship before. There was a lot of lying and cheating on her part, so he was anxious. It was very black and white in my friend's eyes – he believed in full disclosure.

"I don't know, brother. Sometimes the past is best left there." I know that's where I wanted to leave my own.

Craig regarded me for a second before shaking his head. "You haven't said anything to Anna yet, have you?"

I blew out a breath. "No. Don't really see a point. I'm with Christine on this one, brother. It doesn't affect my relationship now and I'm over it, so why bring it up?"

"Seriously?! You're both fucking nuts, you know that? Anna is going to find out at some point and it should be sooner rather than later. I don't know how you can't see that some woman lying to you about being pregnant with your kid, and then lying about losing it, isn't relevant. Especially when you're dating a single mother."

"It isn't. What the fuck man? It doesn't matter anymore. It's over."

The conversation had me fuming. Now I understood why Christine hung up on his stubborn ass.

"Drop it, Craig. You worry about your own shit, okay?"

"Whatever. I'm sick of it anyway. I'm going back to work"

We worked the rest of the day without a word. We both needed to cool off.

It was nearly six when we got done. I shot a quick text to Anna to inform her that I was on my way.

Me: Just got done. Rome ok?

Anna: He's coloring wants to go to the park after dinner k?

Me: Yeah sounds good. Need to blow off some steam anyway

I climbed into the cab of my truck and headed to Anna's. I was glad we had taken both trucks today because I did not feel like putting up with Craig right now.

I was still running what he said through my mind when I pulled up behind Anna's Jeep. Even if he was right about me needing to tell her about Kiersten, how do you bring something like that up? In the end, I let it go for now, not wanting to ruin my night.

I spotted Anna behind the counter, waiting on an older lady. I took the time to really look at her. She had her hair pulled back – she must have been working in her studio earlier – and a bright red tank on, showing off her perfect breasts. I couldn't wait to run my tongue over those again. Hell, I couldn't wait for a lot of things to happen again.

Anna glanced up as the lady walked away and smiled at me. Her smile was something else, I swear it lit up the whole room. I lived for the smiles that were only for me.

"Where's Roman?"

"Oh, he's coloring in the office with Chris. Why don't you let him know you're here? I'm getting ready to close up anyway."

"Sure thing, babe" I pushed through the back door and went into the office. I found Roman sprawled on the floor, crayons scattered around him, and Christine with her head bowed over, studying the papers on the desk. I cleared my throat to announce myself. They both looked up and smiled, making me feel like I belonged here. After the crap with Craig, I needed that.

"How's it going little man? You bein' good for your aunt?"

"'Course I am. Right, Aunt Chris?" He gave her the biggest puppy eyes I had ever seen. Damn, he was good.

"Yeah, of course bud. Best kid ever. How are you doing, Noah?"

"Alright, I guess. Craig and I got into it today. He's up in arms because I agree with you."

She arched her brow in surprise. "You do?"

I raised my chin slightly, and held her stare, "Yeah, Christine, I do. Sometimes there are things from the past that don't matter anymore. While they were tough to go through, if you're over it, well, you're over it." I watched her as she let what I said sink in before continuing. "But, Christine, if you're not over it, if there even is an "it", you might want to think about talking to him."

Christine nodded solemnly at me, taking what I was saying seriously. She cast her eyes down at the desk and took a few deep breaths. After a couple beats she stood up and went over to help Roman clean up. I bent down and saw what he was working on.

"Rome, this looks real good man. Think you could draw something for me to hang up at my place?"

"Really?" He asked with caution, like he couldn't believe what I was saying. "You want one? To take?"

"Yeah man, I sure do."

He jumped up and launched himself into my arms. Roman's arms wrapped around my neck and I melted into a damn puddle. Christine noticed it too, damn it, and did her best to bite back a grin.

"C'mon Rome, let's get upstairs and wait for your momma."

We turned around to leave and just about ran over Anna. She stopped dead at the sight of me holding Roman and all I could do was hope she liked it. I watched her as a smile slowly spread across her face at us – yeah, she liked it.

"I'm just going to check on something in the studio. I'll be up in just a minute, okay?"

"That's fine babe. We were just headin' that way. See you in a bit."

I watched her walk down the hall and absently place her fingertips on something framed on the wall. She didn't even look at it, but it was an obvious habit. Before I could think about it too hard, Roman wiggled in my arms.

As we made our way up the stairs, I couldn't stop wondering what she had touched on the wall. I was going to have to check it out. But for now, I had more important things to do.

Chapter Fourteen

Anna

Summer had flown by and soon I was going to have to get a grip. My baby was going to school, and I was a freaking mess about it. The only person who understood was my mom, and even she said I needed to relax. I know that it's part of life, but I worried that I was losing him. I would blink and he'd be grown.

It was on a last minute trip for school supplies when I finally lost it. Thank goodness Noah had offered to take Roman while I ran to the store. I would have been so embarrassed if he had seen me break down in the parking lot. I couldn't believe that an Iron Man lunch box would cause gut-wrenching sobs, but when I saw it on the passenger seat I could not hold back the tears.

I walked into the apartment thirty minutes later to the sound of Roman laughing hysterically. I found him being pinned to the floor, being tickled by Noah. They hadn't noticed me yet, so I ducked back behind the wall to watch them.

"You still think I'm old Rome? Can an old man take you down like that?"

"Y-y-y-e-e-sss!" Roman squealed gasping for breath.

"I guess you want me to keep tickling you, huh? Come on man, tell me I'm young."

"I taught Roman not to lie, Noah." I said laughing as I came out of hiding.

Both of their heads popped up in surprise. Roman took the opportunity to pull out of Noah's hold and ran to me for a hug. Noah just sat on the floor, smiling at me. It made me feel so special when he looked at me as if I was his whole world.

He watched me for a minute. His stare searched for something, I didn't realize how observant he was until he asked Roman to grab something from his room.

"You okay babe? It looks like you've been crying."

My hands flew to my face, and I glanced at Roman's door. I hoped he hadn't seen through me as easily as Noah. Before I could turn back to him, Noah's arms wrapped around me. With him I knew I was safe cared for.

"Anna, you ok?"

"Yeah, it's nothing." I let out a ragged breath. "I just kind of lost it in the car. This school thing is harder than I thought."

Noah's arms squeezed me with gentleness and affection. He brought one hand up and cupped my chin. Placing a chaste kiss on my lips he leaned back and smiled at me. "It'll be all right. He's growing up, but he still needs his Momma. Don't worry."

His words comforted me. How he knew exactly the right thing to say, I couldn't tell you. But I realized that I was worried Roman wasn't going to need me anymore, which is silly since he still can't tie his shoes.

I placed my hands on the sides of Noah's face and pulled him in for a real kiss.

"Ew! Quit it!"

Noah pulled away, chuckling at Roman. He reached over, ruffled his hair, and tweaked his little nose.

"One day Roman, I'm gonna get to say that to you. You wait."

"No way! Girls are gross!"

"Ok. We'll see. So," Noah turned back to me, "How 'bout we go out tonight? The three of us could use a break from dishes, yeah?"

He pulled me close. His mouth was next to my ear, "We're gonna need a baby sitter soon, Anna. I am going crazy thinking about everything I want to do to you." He nipped at my ear before letting me go.

I definitely needed Roman to spend the night at my parent's house in the near future. Noah and I hadn't gotten but a handful of stolen moments by ourselves. It was frustrating, but he made it clear our first time together was not going to be a quickie before he left for the night. I still wasn't comfortable with him staying over yet, so we were both a little frustrated.

We got to Rinaldi's and were seated immediately. I looked around, trying to be casual, and saw my candlesticks on every table. Kathryn had been pleased with my work, promising to spread the word to whoever would listen. Spotting her at a table near the back, I waved as we walked by. It wasn't a few minutes later that Kathryn joined us.

"Anna, my dear, I have wonderful news. My son is coming for a visit in a few weeks and wants to take a look at your store. He will be buying for a new gallery and I told him about your lovely vases."

"Thank you Kathryn, that sounds wonderful. I finished the window piece last week, have you seen it?"

"Oh yes, it is exquisite. I believe that piece is exactly what Marco is looking for. Would you be willing to part with it so soon?"

The idea that her son might want to buy my piece was surprising. Marco was a big art buyer for luxury hotels and other big corporations. To have him buy one of my pieces to be put on display would be amazing.

"I think I could sell it to the right person, Kathryn. I'll think of something to replace it with, I'm sure."

We chatted for a few more minutes, but my head was swimming at the idea of Marco wanting something of my creation – maybe even more than one.

Kathryn left us when our food arrived. Roman chattered non-stop about school starting, but the news from Kathryn had softened the sting. We were all moving forward as we should.

After we finished, Noah drove us to the park. He and Roman were going nearly three days a week now. I never had to ask if he was coming by. Noah always texted or called in the morning, giving me an idea whether he would be able to make it.

We were all very comfortable with the progression of the relationship. Noah was the missing piece for us. I knew I was far past falling for him, but I was still scared that it could end at anytime. Things happened.

Roman ran off to the slides while Noah came to sit next to me on a bench. He dropped his arm behind me. I leaned into him, breathing in the scent of pine that defined him.

"Big things are gonna happen, babe. That Marco guy would be an idiot to overlook you as a source."

"Mmm. I hope so. I guess we'll find out in a few weeks." I tried to sound nonchalant as if I wasn't fearful of being rejected. I snuggled in closer, pressing myself against Noah's side, craving the stability and comfort that I seemed to only be able to find in his arms.

We stayed like that on the bench until the sun began set. Driving home, I smiled to myself; things were falling into place at last.

***

A few days after our trip to the park, I finally took the time to call my mom. I needed an overnight babysitter, and I needed one now. Every time Noah touched me I felt like I was being set on fire. He knew it, too. He would smirk at my discomfort, adjust his pants, and go on with whatever he was doing.

This had to end. We needed to be alone.

After the second ring, my dad answered the phone. "Hey Dad, how's it going?"

"Good, Banana. Your mom is running me ragged with her honey-do list. How about you, honey? Something on your mind?"

"Oh, things are fine. The store is steady and Roman is excited for school to start."

We chatted for a few minutes about everyday life. I was hesitating. Once I asked for them to keep Roman, and told them why, Noah would be fair game. At least it wasn't my mom on the phone.

"Okay, Anna, what did you really call about?" The man knew me so well.

"I have a date on Friday, and I was hoping you might keep Roman overnight." The words flew out of my mouth so fast and with so much force I was almost shouting.

"Was that so hard?" Was he laughing? My dad was laughing at me. I didn't see the humor. "We can always watch him."

"Thanks Dad. I'll bring him by around six, okay?"

"You'll both bring him. I want to meet this guy, and so will your mother."

I sighed heavily, knowing there was no point in arguing. If they wanted to meet Noah, well, they would find a way. "Fine, Dad. We will be there around six."

A few minutes later we hung up, and I got back to work. Noah would be here soon to take Roman to the park, so I snuck a peak in the mirror on the wall, and stepped out of the office. As I pushed open the door leading into the store, I was smiling, thinking of my upcoming date.

"I hope that smile is for me."

I looked up to my favorite pair of blue eyes twinkling at me. Noah smiled at me and my breath caught in my throat. He was gorgeous.

"In fact, it was. I just got off the phone with my dad. We'll drop Roman off around six on Friday…" I let my voice drift off, nervous of his reaction. My eyes dropped to my shoes while I waited.

"Anna, you okay?"

"I-I-I." I cleared my throat, "I'm fine."

"Right. Is that why your staring at the floor, stuttering? 'Cause you're fine? What's up?"

"Nothing, really. Just, well, my dad wants you to come with me to drop Roman off. It's been a long time since my dad has had to meet a new boyfriend. I don't even know if you want to meet him, or *if* you're my boyfriend. I just didn't want to make you feel weird."

Noah placed his hand over my mouth, effectively cutting off my blubbering. I took a deep breath and looked up again.

"I'm happy to meet your parents."

My body began relax as soon as he spoke the words.

"But I'm not your boyfriend."

And then I went rigid and my heart plummeted. I had read too much into it, into us. I defined what he didn't want to define. I think I even heard myself whimper.

Noah gingerly grasped my chin with his thumb and forefinger. "Anna, I'm not in high school. I'm your man, not your boyfriend. Yeah?"

Noah placed a soft kiss on my lips and I melted into him. "Yeah, okay, Noah." Breathy, I was breathy! Oh the things this man did to me.

As if on cue, Roman pushed the door open, and I pulled myself away from Noah. I hadn't talked to Roman about Noah. I wasn't sure how he would feel about it being more than friendly. Or if he already knew that it was since he had walked in on that one kiss.

"Hey Noah! Ready to go?"

"Yeah, bud, just sayin' hi to your mom."

The admiration for Noah was shining in my boy's eyes. Their relationship made me as nervous as it did happy. What would happen if it ended? How would Roman handle that?

I pushed the thought away. I wasn't going to let negative Anna have her say. She was not in charge, not anymore.

"I'm going to have Christine come out and mind the storefront while you two are gone. I'll probably still be in the studio when you get back."

"Probably? You're always in there." I looked up to see Pete walking in and I at once wondered if something was wrong; it was such an odd time for a visit from him. His eyes went to Noah quickly. They shifted to where Noah was holding Roman's hand and then up at me, filled with questions.

"Rome, who's your friend?" It sounded like such an innocent question, but I knew my brother better than that.

"This is Noah. He's teachin' me football, Unca Pete."

Noah and Pete met halfway, hands extended. There seemed to be a silent yet meaningful guy conversation as they looked each other over while exchanging pleasantries.

"Unca Pete, you wanna come?"

Oh no. I had to intervene. "Roman, I'm sure Uncle Pete is busy and just stopping by. Right, Peter?" I finished through clenched teeth.

"Actually, sis, I have the rest of the day off. I was going to see if Roman wanted to hang out. You guys mind if I tag along?"

I started to object, but was cut off by Noah. "I don't mind if Roman doesn't."

Pete gave me a toothy smile, knowing I was not happy. Now he could give the "big brother" scare a go and I wouldn't be there to stop him.

"Well as long as everyone is okay with it. I'm going to get to work in the studio." I pushed back through the door, desperate to escape my pending embarrassment.

I squeaked – yes squeaked – when a strong hand grabbed my wrist. I spun around and was plastered against Noah's muscular chest. The sight had me at a loss for words.

"You didn't kiss me goodbye, babe."

"Oh, um, well, ah…" And again my blabbering was cut off by his perfect lips. I could kiss him for days.

I deepened the kiss, completely lost in his taste. A low growl came from the back of his throat as I slid my tongue across his bottom lip.

The coolness of the air hit my chest as he pulled away. I missed him instantly.

"I gotta go now before I take you into your studio and embarrass everyone out here."

I was stunned by his words. And the look in his eye told me he wasn't joking. Nodding I started to turn to the studio door.

"You comin', Noah? Or is my sister afraid to leave us alone?" Pete, of course, would interrupt; just because he can I suppose. I gave him a sassy smirk and walked away down the hallway. Ugh, brothers.

Chapter Fifteen

Noah

I watched her walk away, and as I was on the verge of leaving with Pete, when movement caught my eye. Anna gently placed her fingertips on a picture that hung on the wall just before she walked in and shut the door.

She didn't even look up at it, just touched it. There was something in her action that increased my need to see the picture. I moved to go down the hall when a firm hand cupped my shoulder. I turned to see Pete. He seemed almost sad. Like he knew it was a bad idea for me to go look at the picture.

I broke free and walked to the frame. My heart stopped. And then it sunk to the floor. It was the same picture that Roman had on his nightstand. Henry. Fuck.

Without a word, I walked back to the store, grabbed Roman's hand and the three of us walked to the park.

***

Mother fucking Henry ate at me the entire way. Roman was able to tell something was wrong, and I didn't want him to feel bad, so I sucked it up and tossed the ball around with them. Pete was pretty cool, and I could tell that he and Roman were close. It was great that we all seemed to get along well.

Eventually, Roman wanted to run around the playground, and it was just Pete and me. I prepared myself for the big brother shit to start.

"Don't worry about it, man."

I looked at Pete, totally confused. "Worry about what?"

The same sad expression that had crossed his face when I saw that picture was back and I understood. Henry. It was always that motherfucker. I hated him. And I hated that I hated him because he had been important to Anna. But, no matter what anyone said, I felt like I was still fighting a damn ghost. And I could tell Pete knew it.

"He was a big part of her life for a long time, man. To be honest, it was weird they even got together, but it seemed to be good. His death was hard, but I think she mourned for the father Roman didn't get to meet, more than anything. He was a good guy."

Not what I wanted to hear. Part of me wanted him to be an asshole – someone easy to replace. But another part of me – the adult part – was glad Roman had a dad worth remembering.

"Yeah, it just sucks, you know, competing with the memory of him." I can't believe I let that slip. God, I am such a girl.

Pete watched me for a minute, "If you hurt her, I'll have to kick your ass, you know?"

I barked out a laugh, part in surprise at the obvious conversation change, but also because he sounded as if he didn't want to have to do it.

"Roman likes you, and he'll be mad at me if it comes to that, so just don't be an asshole. Are we good?"

I glanced down at his extended hand, grabbing it roughly. "Yeah, man, we're good. If I hurt her or Roman, no one will have to kick my ass. I'll do it myself."

That seemed to satisfy him, and we just talked about normal shit. I found out that Pete owned his own plumbing business and made sure I got his info for future projects.

We hung out until Roman came up to us, begging for food. As we made our way back and dropped Pete off at his office, which was a block from Anna's place, Roman complained about his stomach hurting."I bet your mom has dinner done, don't worry. You'll feel better soon." I picked him up and carried him the rest of the way.

***

It was finally Friday. I was going to get Anna alone – for hours. I could barely concentrate on work without thinking about her. Or what I was going to do to her – with her.

Craig went to visit his family for the weekend (I might have threatened and bribed him) so we would go back to my place tonight. I wanted to take her someplace without memories.

The image of her placing her fingertips on that damn picture was stuck in my head and it killed me. However, Henry would not be a fucking issue tonight. I was going to make sure that her thoughts were solely on her and me.

Bounding up the stairs, taking them two at a time, I think about what I want to say to Roman. He needs to know that he is a part of this and separate all at the same time. As I reached to knock on the door, it opened and the sight hit me hard in the chest. Anna was in front of me more stunning than ever. I can't help looking her over, top to toe.

Her dark hair was down in loose waves, begging for my fingers to thread right through it. She had on a thin, loose tank that almost matched her eyes. Her jeans fit her perfectly, but I needed more. Without a word I pointed my finger up towards the ceiling and motioned for her to spin around. When she did – laughing at me – I could see just how well those jeans fit her perfect ass.

I walked up and placed my hands on her soft hips, giving her a slight squeeze before I placed a kiss right below her ear. Her skin was so soft, I couldn't help but linger, tasting her with a quick slip of my tongue. Her body shivered at the contact and I smiled against her skin. She was just as excited as I was.

We wasted no time getting Roman's things for the night, and we headed over to Anna's parents' house. I could feel the anxiety pulsing out of her on the way. Anna drummed her fingers nervously against her thigh until I grabbed her had. She offered a small smile, and I gripped her tighter, letting her know that everything would be fine.

Anna's parents' house was across town in an older subdivision, but it had been taken care of very well. The front porch appeared freshly painted, with no loose boards that I could feel as I walked across it. The windows had been replaced recently, too. Before we got to the door, it swung open to reveal what could only be described as Anna in thirty years.

"You must be Noah! I'm Anna's momma." I reached out to shake her hand, but was pulled into an excited hug. Quickly releasing me, she scanned me, from the ground up, and gave me an approving smile.

"It's a pleasure to meet you, Mrs. Johnston."

"Oh, none of this 'Mrs. Johnston' stuff. Call me Rose."

"Rose it is, ma'am."

We were shuffled into the house, Roman shooting off somewhere. The inside of the house was what realtors tell me to call "cozy." Anna's parents' living room was filled with comfortable looking older furniture, covered with colorful blankets. The television was in the corner, easy to watch, but not the center focus.

Rose motioned for us to sit, but I had to excuse myself. "I need to find Roman real quick. We need to have a talk – if that's ok." I looked to the two women who were both nodding at me wondering what was going on. I walked the way Roman had left, finding him on the back porch petting an older dog. The dog just lifted his eyes at me and went back to sleep. This was as good a place as any. I sat down next to him on the porch.

"Roman, you know I'm taking your momma on a date tonight, right?"

That got me a slow nod. Okay, step one – done.

"I want to talk to you about it for a minute. Is that okay?"

He nodded again, telling me that he was just as nervous as I was.

"Well, Rome, I need you to know something. It's really important." I cleared my throat, surprised at how emotional this was making me.

"Rome, whatever happens with me and your momma, well, it doesn't change me being your friend. Yeah? No matter what, I'll still hang out with you; help you with sports, or whatever, for as long as you want me around. Does that sound good?"

I waited for him to say something for a long time. When he was ready, he would answer me.

"I wanna be your friend too. My friend Caleb's momma dated this guy. He liked him a whole lot. Then one day he just went away. You're not gonna go away are you?" Roman looked up at me, fear written across his little face. My gut clenched at the thought of leaving him even though I knew I wouldn't.

"No way, little man. We are friends outside of anything that happens with your momma. Friends stick together, right?" I barely got the last word out before he leapt into my arms, almost knocking me on my back. He wrapped his arms around my neck for a solid minute before backing off.

I placed a hand on his shoulder and gave it a squeeze. "I'm gonna go take your momma out now, okay? So, I'll see you in a few days."

Roman smiled brightly at me, no trace of concern could be found. "Okay, Noah. Have fun!"

With that he sat back down and went back to petting the dog. I stood up and moved to go back in the house, only to be confronted by a large older version of Pete standing in the doorway. Anna's father could probably scare most men just standing there. Good thing I'm not most men.

"I don't mean to pry, but I heard a bit of what you said to my grandson. I sure hope you're up for that friendship, son." Anna's father held my stare with a seriousness only found in protective fathers.

Looking him in the eye, unwavering in my conviction, I admitted, "Wouldn't give it up for anything, sir."

"Good to hear. You must be Noah. I'm Mitchell Johnston, glad to meet you." He extended his hand and grabbed mine firmly. He was definitely not a dad to mess with.

"Noah Evans, sir. Sorry it took so long to get out here to meet you."

"Oh, I'm betting that has more to do with Anna than you." His lips quirked at me and I understood he was close with his daughter and he knew she was scared to bring new people into her life.

We walked back to our women who were still talking in the living room. Anna stood up, and I reached for her hand. Lacing my fingers with hers, I leaned over and placed my lips next to her ear, "I had my talk with Roman, so I'm ready if you are."

Anna leaned back a few inches and tilted her head. With a raised eyebrow she asked, "Are you going to tell me what that was about?"

Mitchell answered before I could, "It was a man's conversation, Banana, leave it alone." Anna glared at her father, snapping her mouth shut with a click of her teeth. Damn, I liked this guy.

We said our goodbyes and walked out to the truck. I knew Anna was curious about my conversation with Roman, but she was wise enough to listen to her dad and let it go.

We got to the restaurant thirty minutes later. It was one owned by Kathryn Rinaldi in Charleston. I knew Anna loved the place in town, so I figured this was the way to go. Judging by Anna's broad smile when we pulled up, I had made a good choice.

We ate over candlesticks from Kiln Me Now – something that made her even happier – and got to know each other better. I learned that she had been afraid of heights until Pete dared her to go skydiving, and before she fell in love with pottery she had thought about becoming a nurse like her mother. I told her how I worked with my dad at a young age, learning how to bring life back into old homes. Anna told me how hard it had been for her when Christine had left for college and how she started Kiln Me Now. She also told me a lot about Roman as a baby though she was careful to not bring up Henry. Whether that was for my sake or hers, I couldn't tell.

Everything was perfect. Well, almost perfect. Craig's voice kept popping up in my head, telling me to tell Anna about Kiersten. I pushed the thought back though, not wanting to ruin the night. I would tell her – just not now.

We drove around after dinner, enjoying the sights of the striking city. Eventually I made my way back to Franklin. She turned her body to face me when we passed her street, "Where are we going, Noah?"

I needed to see her reaction, so I shifted to see her while gripping the wheel. "My place."

"Oh. Okay." She nervously looked out the window, her hands fidgeting. I hoped it was excitement and not cold feet because I didn't know what I would do if she wasn't ready for this.

Stopping the truck in my parking spot, I jumped out to get Anna's door. She took my hand and looked at me with a shy, but sexy smile. Well, there went my question about cold feet. Anna was nervous, sure, but without a doubt willing. I wrapped my arm around her waist and led her down the sidewalk. We made our way to my apartment, and I got her comfortable on the couch.

"You want a beer or anything?" Oh, please say no.

"No, I'm fine." She patted her hand on the spot next to her, and like a high school virgin, I all but threw myself down next to her.

"Thank you for tonight, Noah. It's been forever since I had one this amazing."

"We'll have to do it again then, yeah?"

"Absolutely." She said while staring at my lips and when her tongue peeked out to wet her bottom lip my restraint broke. I reached my hand behind her head, threading my fingers into her hair, and pulled her close. A slight gasp escaped her and as she opened her mouth a fraction, I took the opportunity to slide my tongue in.

The taste of her took over my mind and body and I couldn't get enough of it. Plundering her perfect mouth wasn't enough though; I needed to taste every inch of her. As if it has a mind of its own, my other hand skimmed the hem of her shirt, sliding underneath it.

I heard her release a soft moan as I traced my fingertips up her side. Finding my way to the lace of her bra, I gently brushed my thumb over her nipple. I could feel it hard and aching under the fabric. Anna leaned in to my touch, one of her hands diving into my hair, the other to my stomach. We went at it like teenagers for what seemed like forever. Finally, with my dick screaming for relief, I placed my hands under her, lifting her as I stood.

Anna's long legs wrapped around my waist, her hands held my head firmly to hers careful to never break our kiss. I blindly walked to my bedroom, ready to strip and devour her. I placed her on top of my bed, lifting her shirt as I set her down. She sucked her bottom lip into her mouth and her teeth sunk into it. I grabbed the back of my own shirt and pulled it over my head, tossing it to the side. As I started to unbutton my jeans, Anna's fingers covered mine, moving them out of the way. Her eyes were filled with conflicting emotions. She wanted to run the show, to feel empowered and sexy – who was I to deny her that?

I let her take control, for now. My jeans slid down my legs, her hands brushing against me while they pushed the stiff fabric. I kicked them off and leaned over her. As she lay back, I worked open her pants with one hand. Anna raised her hips slightly, allowing me to tug them off the rest of the way. I stared at her, looking so sexy on my bed in her white lace. She graced me with a seductive smile, beckoning me with her finger to come closer.

Pressing my body down on hers, I pulled her covered breast into my mouth. Her nipple pressed against the fabric, straining to be freed. Running my fingers along the strap toward the full cups, I pulled the lace down. I licked and sucked the tight bud while she thrashed beneath me. I released her with a pop and moved to the other one. Anna pressed her hips to mine, begging for friction to ease her need.

I settled between her legs, pressing my rock-hard cock into her heat. She let out a whimper, and I swear I got harder. I kissed and licked my way up her neck and captured her lips. I rolled her over, enjoying the sight of her on top of me as I unclasped her bra. I watched as she let it fall, hitting me in the chest lightly. Anna leaned down, grinding my cock and licking my neck.

She moved her way down to my chest before I realized her intent. I fought the urge to stay quiet and take whatever she gave me, but I couldn't do it. "Anna, babe, you don't have to."

"I want to. I need to feel you in my mouth before I feel you anywhere else."

Only a stupid man would argue, and I am not a stupid man. I moved, so she was next to me as she kissed and licked her way down my stomach. With graceful hands she reached my boxer-briefs. She grasped my cock and pulled it free, rubbing her thumb across the bead of pre-cum that appeared on the slit. Her eyes grew slightly as she realized my size. I couldn't help but smirk at her and raise my eyebrows. She retaliated by sliding her tongue from my balls all the way up the vein back to my swollen head.

"Fuck, Anna. You're gonna kill me." I groaned as my eyes rolled back.

She laughed as I pulled my hips up, helping her remove my underwear. As soon as I kicked them off, her tongue was swirling around the head of my dick and I was sliding my fingers through her hair. Anna made her way up the bed until she was next to me on her hands and knees. She bent her head down and kissed my stomach, the sensation had my muscles coiled tight in anticipation.

Determined to let her take the lead, I removed my hand before I pushed her head down. I skimmed her back, resting my hand on her ass as she wrapped her hand around my base, squeezing. I ran my finger along the edge of her panties and moved them out of the way when I reached the apex of her thighs. As she sucked me in as far as she could, I pushed the fabric out of the way and inserted two fingers. I matched Anna's rhythm and circled her clit with my thumb as she took her other hand and massaged my balls. I heard and felt her purr as I thrust my fingers in and out of her soaked channel.

Anna released me as I removed my fingers and wrapped my arm around her waist, pulling her under me. My tongue licked a path from her neck, over her tightly budded nipples to her stomach. Her breath hitched as I tugged her panties down. I made a trail of kisses down her legs, pulling the scrap of lace off completely and then made my way back up, kissing, licking, and biting as I went.

I could smell her arousal and it drove me crazy. I licked her sweet pussy bottom to top, sucking her clit in my mouth. I felt her legs shake as I inserted two fingers into her. Anna's moans directed me, telling me what she wanted without the words I knew she couldn't form. I curled my fingers and found her magic spot while my tongue continued to lap up everything she could give me. She clenched around my thrusting fingers as I licked and sucked, pushing her farther and farther.

"Oh, shit, Noah. I'm gonna come." She yelled and bucked, but I held her tight, feeling her pulse around my tongue and fingers. I watched her slowly come down, breathing ragged and her face flushed.

I crawled up her body, reached over and grabbed a foil packet from the nightstand, ripping it open with my teeth. I sat up while Anna watched me roll it over myself, fire burning in her eyes. I rubbed my rough hands up her thighs and waist. I hovered over her, aching to be inside. My cock was at her entrance, begging to play. I pushed myself into her, careful to give her time to stretch around me.

Her eyes closed at the movement. I couldn't let her do that. I needed to know she was with me, only me. "Look at me, Anna. Eyes open and on me."

They snapped open and held my stare. I pulled out a few inches only to push back in deeper. Anna's hips tilted as I pushed, forcing me in farther. As a moan escaped her, I pushed myself the entire way in and stopped. If I moved right then I would embarrass myself thoroughly. She moved her hips slightly, and I pushed my weight down, pinning her still.

"Damn, Anna, you're so fucking perfect. Just give me a second or this won't last."

"Please Noah, you have to move. I'm so close." She whispered her demand, begging me to relieve her.

Slowly, I started rocking back and forth, in and out, as her tight pussy held me like a vice. I slammed my mouth over hers, my tongue mimicking my dick. Over and over until I could feel her body going tighter, ready to explode.

"Noah!"

The best sound in the world was her screaming my name as her pussy pulsed around my cock. The muscles clenched over and over until they drove me to my own release. Our eyes stayed locked the entire time. I dropped down next to her on the bed and pulled her back to my front. Holding her like this felt exactly how I thought it would. It was right; complete. This was where I wanted to be.

We stayed that way for a while, quietly soaking up the emotions running between us. With reluctance, I left to dispose of the condom, but hurried back to her, not wanting to miss out on any of our time together. I needed to use tonight to mark her, claim her, and ruin her for anyone else. Anna was mine now. If she had any doubts, I planned on erasing them tonight.

I found her with the sheet pulled up over her breasts. I couldn't let her cover up the very thing I had been craving for weeks. I gave it a quick tug, revealing her perfect body. She looked at me smiling, "I was cold, caveman."

"I'll keep you warm. Don't worry." I replied with a smirk.

"I have no doubt. But first, I'm going to clean up." I watched her walk away, naked and sexy as hell. She wasn't gone long. Returning to the bed, she pressed her body against me. Wrapping my arms around her, I settle.

Eventually, Anna's breathing became shallow and even, telling me she fell asleep. I held her a little tighter and let sleep claim me too.

Chapter Sixteen

Noah

Waking up with Anna in my arms is everything I thought it would be. After last night I can't imagine letting her go, but I know I have to. She will want to let Roman get used to us. Hell, what if she won't let me stay until we're married? Whoa, hold on a second, married? Where the hell did that come from? It had only been a few months, so there is no need to get ahead of myself. But the thought of marrying Anna and being Roman's dad, doesn't scare me. I thought after everything Kiersten put me through it would be a long fucking time before I would think about forever with someone. But, I didn't know Anna then, and my girl isn't anything like that bitch. Anna is pure goodness, through and through. I was falling for her hard and fast – which was how I would take her this morning.

I slid my hand over her hip, stroking her side. Reaching for her full breast I massage it, brushing my thumb across her peaked nipple. I heard her breathing change as she woke up. She feigned sleep for a few minutes as I continued to roam her body. Finally giving in to my demands, she turned, clutching my cock in her firm grip.

Her hand stroked me from base to tip until I was almost ready to explode. In one fluid motion, Anna was on top of me and sliding down my cock.

I groaned, "Fuck babe, we need a condom."

"Just a minute, this feels too good."

She wasn't wrong. It felt like we were made for each other – fitting together perfectly, I held back, stilling myself, so she could ride out her building orgasm.

She pulled me out and started to reach into the drawer, stopping halfway. Before I could ask what was wrong, she spun her body around and had my dick practically down her throat. The shock of it had me on the verge of losing control within minutes. The combination of her hot, wet mouth and knowing she could taste herself mixed with me was my undoing.

"Anna, stop or I'm going to come."

Her answer was to suck harder, making my vision darken. I stuck my hand into her hair, bucking my hips as I pulsed hot cum into her mouth. I squeezed my eyes shut as stars exploded behind my lids, bursting with each pulse. Anna sucked me dry, leaving me a limp and worthless pile of flesh. She gave me a dreamy smile as I rubbed my thumb across her lips. "We taste really damn good, Noah."

Holy shit, that dirty talk coming out of my Anna was hot. I flipped her over and licked her from the base of her ear, over her breasts, down her stomach, and finally her sweet lower lips. As always, just the sweet flavor of her caused me to get hard, even with the blow job to end all blow jobs I just received. The heat from Anna's core enveloped my fingers as I plunged them into her. My tongue flicked and licked her clit as I continued to bring her to and over the edge. Each whimper and moan made me harder. Desire and need filled my entire body. Unable to stand it any longer, I pushed myself up away from Anna, causing her to whimper in protest. I ripped a condom off of the nightstand and got it on in record time. With little restraint I grabbed her wrists and held them above her head as I sunk myself into her slick, tight pussy. I held her in place, impaling her with each thrust I took her just as I had originally planned this morning – hard and fast.

I came with a roar as she screamed my name in her own release. I lay down next to Anna, pulling her close – placing her in the crook of my arm, her head on my chest. We laid there in the quiet for a while as her fingers played with the hair on my chest.

"What do you plan to do today?" I asked, not wanting to end our time together. I just got her where I wanted her and I selfishly didn't want to give that up.

"The store opens at ten this morning, so I'll need to go home and get ready for that. Mom will bring Roman home sometime later in the afternoon. What about you?"

"I could go work on the house. Craig's gone until the afternoon, so that would give me time to sand the floors."

Neither of us made any effort to leave the bed for a while. Finally, Anna shifted and went into the bathroom. I forced myself to get up too and gathered our clothes, placing mine in the hamper and hers on the bed. I got dressed and went to the kitchen to make coffee. Rummaging through our empty cabinets for something to eat, I realized how often I was eating at Anna's. I reminded myself to make sure I filled both of our cabinets.

I was pouring coffee as Anna walked in wearing my shirt. She looked so fucking sexy in my clothes. I grabbed a handful of my shirt and tugged her close.

"Is this okay? I can change…" Her voice was filled with doubt.

"Babe, it's more than okay. You are fucking hot in my shirt. The sight makes me wanna rip it off of you though."

She smiled at me and took the cup I offered. We milled around for a few minutes, drinking coffee, savoring being alone just a little longer. It would be over soon enough.

Chapter Seventeen

Anna

After an amazing night with Noah, I was reluctant to go home, but the store had to open and I needed to get ready. Noah drove me home, holding my hand the entire way. I was grateful for that – I wasn't ready to lose that connection with him. I had never felt like this about anyone. I was so afraid of falling for Noah; I missed when it happened. But after last night I knew I was hopelessly in love with him.

The admission scared the hell out of me though. The power to completely crush me was held firmly in his hands. And Roman! How would he handle it if something went wrong? The thought of Roman had me wondering what their conversation was about. I know my dad wanted me to let it be between them, but as his mother, I should have been told.

When we got into my apartment I finally got the guts to ask. "What did you and Roman talk about last night?"

His eyes slid over to me while he smiled, opening the door. "It's between me and him, babe."

"Not good enough. I have the right to know." I was snippy, and I hated it, but I had to know what it was all about. I sat down on the couch in a huff.

Sitting next to me he drawled, "Well, since you asked so nicely. I wanted to let Roman know that no matter what happens between you and me, I would always be his friend."

My heart swelled at his words. Pin pricks started at the backs of my eyes and before I could stop it, a tear escaped, sliding down my cheek.

Noah cupped my cheek and swiped the tear away. A mask of worry covered his face. "What's wrong? I didn't mean that I thought something would happen. Talk to me, babe. Did I overstep?"

I inhaled slowly, trying to formulate the words, but only sobs came out. Noah wrapped his arms around me, rocking gently.

After a few minutes, I got myself together and pulled out of his embrace. He watched me warily, probably wondering if my crying jag was over.

"I'm sorry. I don't know what came over me. That was so thoughtful of you. Roman really loves your time together. I guess knowing you respected him enough to address concerns about that – well it means a lot."

My honestly was rewarded with a full-blown smile and a hard kiss on the mouth. This man really knew how to take my breath away. I knew I needed to get ready, but just one touch from Noah had me igniting. As if he could read my thoughts, he pulled back. "Don't have enough time for that, babe."

"Ugh, I know. I'm going to jump in the shower, if you don't have anywhere to be, you can hang out until the store opens."

"I'll go make some more coffee, you go get ready. I've got nowhere else I want to be."

I made my way to my room and got busy. After showering and dressing, I put my hair in a thick braid that hung down my back; I did not have the patience to deal with it today. I found Noah staring out the window that over-looked the street, drinking coffee. I wrapped my arms around him from behind, pressing my chest into his muscular back. I could feel his defined abs through the thin cotton of his shirt.

His free hand came up to cover mine and his thumb lightly rubbed my knuckles. We stood there in a comfortable silence until Noah finished his coffee. He turned around in my arms and kissed me on top of my head, "Let's get something to eat before you start your day, yeah?"

"Yeah, that sounds good. I need some coffee, too."

The whole thing flowed effortlessly. We worked together gathering breakfast – talking, laughing, as if we had been doing it for years; as if we would be doing it for years.

***

The store was busy for the next week. Orders went out and new customers came in constantly. Christine had to work the floor, and I needed to work in the studio to keep up. She seemed to appreciate the distraction, though, since she and Craig hadn't spoken more than a handful of words to each other that I knew of. He had dropped by with Noah one day on the way to pick up supplies and the tension between

Craig and my sister was thick – both wanting to talk to the other, but neither willing to make the first move. I needed to make time to talk to her, soon.

Noah and Roman were making use of the last few days of summer vacation by heading to the park more often. I was grateful for the extra time to work without distraction. I was barely keeping up with everything even now that I had a little more help. Marco's visit was next week, and I wanted to create a portfolio for him to look through when he got here. I had to make sure I put my best foot forward.

Between the store, the upcoming meeting (one that still didn't have a specific meeting time), and Romans first day of school on the horizon, I was completely overwhelmed. I shut the door to the studio behind me, exhaustion winning out. I looked up at the picture of Henry and Roman on the wall, smiling. He would be so happy that I found someone so special. And if Henry couldn't be here, he would want someone that cared for Roman as much as Noah soobviously did.

I looked up when I heard Roman burst through the door and run up the stairs. Noah was standing there – his eyes hard and lips pressed in a thin, angry line. Had something happened at the park? I moved to him, wrapping my hand around as much of his large bicep as I could, and rose up on my toes to kiss his cheek.

"Everything go okay? You look upset."

He cleared his throat before answering. "It's fine. Nothing you need to worry about."

His words were meant to comfort, but his voice sounded pained and angry. I figured he would tell me when he wanted to – there was no prying anything out of Noah – so I made my way to the stairs, pulling him to follow me. Noah glanced down the hall one last time before giving in.

We found Roman in the kitchen, pulling out odds and ends from the cabinet. Scanning the counter I saw the makings of peanut butter and jelly sandwiches. Apparently Roman got to pick dinner tonight.

The guys worked together and "dinner" was ready in no time. Noah started off quiet, but the tension seemed to release from him throughout the evening. By the time the dishes were put away he was laughing hysterically while tickling Roman on the couch. I watched them for a few minutes, just soaking in the scene. Noah looked up and caught me staring. The emotions that filled his eyes said more than any words could. It was right then that I knew, without a doubt, that he was falling just as fast as I was. Our gaze stayed locked for almost a full minute, only breaking with the ringing of the phone. I was reluctant to answer it, not wanting to disturb our time.

"Hello?"

"Anna Johnston? This is Marco Rinaldi, Kathryn's son."

Holy shit. Holy shit! He was calling, it was real! I quickly schooled my features and walked to the bedroom, feeling Noah's eyes on me the entire way.

"Mr. Rinaldi, how are you?"

"I am doing well, thank you. I was calling to see if we could set up a time to meet. I have seen some of your work and I think you might be just the artist I need for some commissioned work."

"I-I-I," I took a shaky breath and to be control of myself. "I would love to when are you going to be in town?"

"Will Wednesday work for you? Say, six thirty?"

"Yes, I can make that work, would you like to meet at my store or maybe your mother's restaurant?"

"Ah, great idea! We can talk over dinner, two birds and all that. Sound's good Anna, I'll see you then."

I said my goodbyes and hung up the phone. I stared at it for a moment, in complete shock. I never thought I would have the opportunity to sell my work on such a scale. I was lost in thought when two large arms wrapped around me from behind.

"Good news?"

"That was Marco. We have a meeting on Wednesday evening." My eyes widened as something dawned on me. "Noah, can you stay with Roman? I'm sorry I didn't even think about it when I set it up. Never mind, I should ask Christine. Forget I asked." The words flew out of my mouth faster than I could think in my state of mind.

"No." He stated firmly.

I turned slowly, confusion written all over my face. At least it made him smile.

"No, I will not forget it. No, you will not ask Christine. We're a team, okay? I've got Roman, don't worry about us."

Warmth filled me. 'We're a team.' God, I missed being a part of something like this. Noah bent down and placed a soft kiss on my forehead.

"Roman asked me to put him to bed tonight. That okay with you, babe?"

"Yeah, I think that would be just perfect."

I missed Noah's embrace as he left the room to get Roman ready. I took the opportunity to dream a bit. I pictured us, years from now. Noah helping Roman with homework. Holding our baby. Making love to me every night. The future looked bright for us.

When all of our good nights were said and Roman finally fell asleep, I couldn't hold myself back any longer. Noah and I hadn't been together since our first night, and I needed him.

Taking him by the hand, I led him into my bedroom. Once inside, I turned and locked the door. Noah pressed into me from behind, my hands bracing the door. "I've been dreaming of this, babe. I can't fuck you hard 'cause you'd wake Roman, but I need to be inside you." His voice was rough and filled with lust.

I whimpered as he kissed and sucked my neck. I started to grind my ass into his prominent erection and he rewarded me with a growl. Noah's fingers pressed hard into my hips, pulling me into him. Suddenly, Noah spun me around and our lips crashed together. The taste of him exploded in my mouth. Our tongues danced together, probing with urgency. I forced myself to pull back. Noah looked at me confused at my reaction. "I need to lock the bathroom door."

Without warning, I was lifted and tossed onto the bed as if I was weightless. Noah laughed at my shock. "I'll get the lock. You get naked and spread yourself out on the bed. "

I stripped in record time, not wanting to disappoint him. I laid myself down on the bed, bare to him. He turned to me and stopped. I started to pull the blanket over my body, uncomfortable with the scrutiny. "No way, babe. I want to inspect what's mine. Do not hide yourself from me."

"It seems unfair, Noah. Here I am on display while you are still fully dressed."

"You want me to undress?"

I nodded at him with my brows raised. I was about to smart off to him when he started talking, "Tell you what. You do something for me and I'll strip for you."

"Oh, what's that?" I couldn't help but sound annoyed.

"I want to watch you play with yourself. You do that for me, and I'll take off my clothes at your command."

I should have been embarrassed. I had never done this before for an audience, but the fire in his eyes had me sliding my hand over my breast and down my stomach. I couldn't take my eyes from his as my fingers slowly made their way down. Moisture pooled between my thighs, all but dripping onto the bed. I reached my destination and gingerly circled my clit. As a moan escaped me, I remembered my goal.

With a shaky voice that was filled with need, I had him start to get rid of his clothes. "Noah, remove your shirt."

He reached over his head and pulled the tee shirt over the front – damn that was hot. I slid my finger between my slick folds and my other hand came up to my mouth. I stuck my finger in, slowly pulling it out. As I reached down and rolled my pebbled nipples, Noah let out a desperate sound. It felt good to be able to torture him. I felt empowered and sexy.

"Lose the pants." I could barely get the words out between pants.

Noah undid his buttons and pushed down his jeans and to my surprise he had nothing on underneath. His cock was fully engorged as he fisted it. His eyes didn't leave mine as I swirled my fingers, dipping them into my soaked channel. Noah stalked across the room to me, pumping his hand with each step. He stood between my legs, crawling onto the bed. Still massaging myself, the entire scene became even more erotic when Noah's tongue traced a path up my leg, starting at my ankle.

I had to bit my lip to keep from yelling out. Noah took my hand in his and made his way to the apex of my thighs. He sucked my fingers into his mouth and moaned. My other hand kept rolling and pinching my nipple, causing my body to tremble. I fisted Noah's hair, giving it a slight tug.

"Fuck, Anna, I can't get enough of you," he whispered against me as he licked from the bottom of my slit to the top. "Your pussy is so fucking sweet." He sucked hard on my clit and inserted a thick finger into me. My head thrashed back and forth as my hips bucked at the sensation. Noah held on, his rhythm never wavering.

He licked and sucked my lower lips and clit as his finger pushed in and out of my hot, soaked sex. My body was tight with tension, the orgasm building steadily. When Noah inserted a second finger as he sucked my clit hard, I shattered into a million pieces. Wave after wave pulsed through my body. Noah lapped up all I had to offer, never slowing his movements. I floated for a few minutes as Noah finally brought me down gently. When I was finally able to open my eyes, Noah was crawling up my body, leaving a trail of licks, kisses, and nips in his wake. He reached my face and dipped his tongue into my waiting mouth. The mixture of his taste and mine overwhelmed me. We drowned each other in kisses, and as he lifted himself from me, I nipped at his jaw.

"Give me a second, babe. I gotta grab something." He pulled a foil packet from his jeans pocket and I raised my brow at him. "Hey, I've been prepared since our first night. I never knew when we'd get a chance and didn't want to miss out."

I started to giggle at him, but when he ripped the condom open with his teeth and stroked himself, all humor was gone. In its place was passion and need.

I watched Noah roll the cover over himself, and wetness gathered again. The image of him touching himself was inspiring. Smirking at my obvious need for him, Noah settled between my legs, the head of his steel-like cock at my entrance. Inch by inch he filled me. He pulled his cock out slightly and I whimpered, desperately needing more. Noah moved in and out of me, deeper each time, until he was sheathed to the hilt. Then he stilled, allowing me to stretch to meet his girth. Slowly, he worked himself in and out. Noah dipped his head and pulled my nipple into his mouth. His tongue made circles around my bud before he bit down. The pleasure-pain sent electricity straight to my womb. We were moving in tandem, hands roaming and clawing, tongues caressing, teeth nipping.

The emotions swirling around us were intense, adding to our physical pleasure. There was no mistaking what we were doing. Noah was claiming me, ruining me for any other. This was love making, plain and simple. I didn't have time to consider what it meant when Noah picked up his pace, pushing us over the edge. My legs wrapped around him, pulling him in further. Noah slid his hands under my ass, tilting me slightly. The change in angle sent waves of pleasure through me, causing me to convulse around him. I bit back my moans, still aware of the sleeping body in the next room. Noah followed me with a quiet grunt seconds later, his head in the crook of my neck.

We stayed like that as we caught our breath, exhausted. Noah lifted himself up with his forearms. As he pulled out I felt sadness for losing our physical connection. He lay down next to me, wrapping me in his arms.

"Better than I remembered, babe. That was worth waiting for."

"Oh, yeah, that was amazing."

"Let me take care of this, I'll be right back."

Noah got up and quietly opened the bathroom door. I grabbed his shirt and nearly had it on when I realized he would need it to leave. And he had to leave – I wouldn't know how to explain Noah still being here in the morning to Roman.

I pulled thin cotton pants on as Noah returned. He tilted his head in question at me. I closed my eyes, needing to ask him to leave, but not ready for him to go.

"Talk to me, Anna. What's going on? You look upset. Did I hurt you?"

My eyes popped open in surprise, "God, no! You were perfect. I just." I hesitated, not wanting to put a cloud over what just happened. "I'm not ready for you to go, yet."

"But I need to go, is that what you mean?"

"I'm sorry, yes." Tears threatened to spill down my cheeks as I admitted it. "I'm not ready for you to stay. I'm sorry."

I expected him to be mad and storm out. I expected him to yell and scream, forcing me to explain myself. I did not expect him to grasp my chin with his thumb and forefinger and place a soft kiss on my lips. No, I was shocked by that. Why, though, I wasn't sure. Noah seemed to always know what I was thinking before I did – and when it came to Roman, he didn't push me. I looked into Noah's eyes, swirling with understanding, compassion, and an emotion I couldn't quite decipher.

"I understand, Anna. We take it slow, especially for Roman. But you need know something," he paused, stroking my chin with his callused thumb. "I miss waking up to you. I am looking forward to having that again. Now, put my shirt on."

Do what? My face betrayed my confusion and Noah barked out a short laugh. "Anna, it's still warm enough outside that I won't need it to get home. But I do need to know that you're in it because that is so damn sexy. That picture in my head will make up for not being here with you."

With a goofy grin plastered on my face, I slipped Noah's tee shirt over my head. A few minutes later he was on his way home and I was in bed – my goofy grin still in place.

Chapter Eighteen

Anna

Waking up the next morning was awful. I wanted Noah with me. Hell, I always wanted Noah with me, but we needed to take our time and get to know each other before he was more than a friend to Roman. I didn't even really know if he wanted to be more than that. We didn't talk about it – well I avoided it for the most part.

Roman and I got ready for our day quietly. He was going to spend the day at a friend's house while they still could. School was starting in a few days and he wanted to get as much fun in as possible. That could be tough being in the office most of the time.

I wanted to talk to Christine about Noah, but unless we are working, she is nowhere to be found most days. It was more important to find out what that was about than to complain about guy problems.

I was determined to find out what was going on, so I had called my Mom to help in the store on her day off for a few hours. My Mom was a nurse at the local clinic – had been for thirty years – and took off every other Friday. I was waiting for her to show up when Christine ducked into the office.

To my surprise, my Dad walked through the door as I was dusting the center island. He was wearing an old Kiln Me Now tee shirt that stretched tight across his chest and faded blue jeans. He looked like a bull in a china shop – well, pottery store – being well over six feet tall and heavily muscled. I smiled and went to him, needing a comforting hug.

"Hey Daddy, what are you doing here?"

"Your Mom said you needed help today, and the clinic had someone call in sick. I'm all yours," he said with a full smile.

"Well, I'm glad you're here. I need your advice."

"Let's have at it, Banana. Then you can get to Christine."

My brows shot up in surprise. How did he know?

"She hasn't been by lately, I figured something was bothering her and she was hiding. You needed your Mom just to get some time, and I can put two and two together. So, what's up?"

"Well, Noah and I have begun to get pretty serious, but I'm still nervous about letting him become a big part of Roman's life, of our life."

"Anna that man couldn't be more a part of Rome's life unless you got married. That boy is with Noah more than he is with me and Peter combined. What are you really worried about?"

I stared at my Dad for a moment – he let me mull things over until I was ready. Noah was with Roman at least four days a week. I wasn't really holding them back or keeping them separated, was I?

"Me." I didn't mean to say it out loud, but it slipped out. "I am so selfish. I was so worried about me I never paid attention to how close Roman had gotten to Noah. What have I done? What if he leaves? Or worse." I was stopped abruptly by my father's large hand clamping down over my mouth.

"Banana, breathe. Now I'm going to lift my hand, but that mouth stays shut, you hear me?" I looked at my Dad, his face a mixture of impatience and concern, and nodded.

"Anna, you are not selfish. If I thought Noah was a bad influence on that boy or that he would leave you high and dry, I would have said something. Now, you need to understand something, we do not know the future. We cannot control it either. Hiding yourself away, the same thing you are about to talk to your sister about doing mind you, is not the answer. You and Noah have a shot at something good. He really cares about our boy. A man wouldn't take the kind of time he does for no reason. You and Roman are his reason. I know how men work, baby girl, and he is in this for the long haul – whether or not you are going to embrace it is up to you. So, what are you going to do?"

My Dad is the best at advice. Straightforward and honest, he tells you what you need to hear. So, the question is, what am I going to do? "I don't know Dad. I think…I think it's time. He's worth the risk. Noah is, God Dad, he's amazing, isn't he?"

"I haven't spent a lot of time with him, but based on what Roman says – and that is a lot – that man is just about perfect."

We laughed together over Noah's rock star status in Roman's world. I settled on the decision I had just made, and a sense of calm washed over me. Then my eyes slid to the back door of the store. The calm feeling fled and worry replaced it.

"Go to her, Anna. But be gentle. I don't know what's going on, but she is hurting."

I nodded at my mind-reading father and gave him one last hug. I stepped into the office to find Christine spinning her phone on the desk. Her head shot up and the sadness on her face broke my heart. I moved to her quickly, throwing my arms around her neck.

"Talk to me, Chris. What is going on?"

"I just – I just miss him. I don't know what to do." With a deep breath, Christine burst into long overdue tears. I ran my hand along her back shushing and telling her to breathe. After she calmed down, I released her and sat on the desk.

"You need to call him. He misses you too, Chris. Noah sees it. Hell, I see it. You need to be the one to open the lines of communication this time."

"Do you think he'll even pick up? I've avoided his calls for, geez, it's been weeks."

"I think if you called him right now he would not only pick up, he would stop whatever he was doing and meet you somewhere."

She stared at me dumbfounded for a few seconds. Blinking her eyes a few times, she looked to her phone and then back at me. "I might need to take the rest of the day off, Anna. Would that be alright?"

"Take it. No matter what happens. But Chris," I caught her eye, pleading for an answer, "*are* you keeping something from Craig? From me?"

Her eyes widened – whether in surprise at my question or guilt I couldn't tell. I waited for a few beats before shaking my head at her. "It's okay, you know. You don't have to tell me everything. Just know that you can, ok?"

Christine nodded at me and started to call Craig. I shut the office door on my way out to give her some privacy. Now I understood Craig's reaction. My sister was holding something back – though I couldn't imagine what it was. While I wanted to know, I hoped she would at least talk to Craig. They needed that if their relationship was going to stand a chance.

I had wanted to get some more pieces done to get stocked back up on inventory, but now decided against it. I went back into the store and found my Dad ringing up a customer. The sight reminded me how amazing my family has been; it was nice to have someone willing to help whenever I needed it. I waited until he was done and we were alone to approach him.

"Hey Dad, I think we're good now. I don't know any more than I did, but she's in a better place. If you want to go you can."

"Okay, Banana, I'll see you later." He hugged me and went to the door and stopped suddenly. "Before I forget, your Mom wants everyone for dinner sometime."

"I'll let Pete and Christine know, Dad."

He nodded and pushed through the door. I wondered if this dinner would be a good step forward with Noah. I decided to call my Mom later and ask if it was alright to bring him – though I couldn't imagine she would say no. Hell, she'd probably jump for joy.

About twenty minutes later I heard the back door slam and Christine's car start. I hoped that she and Craig could start over – anyone could see that they were perfect together.

I was preparing my portfolio for my meeting with Marco when he called. Marco explained that one of the hoteliers wanted to join the meeting as well. Marco even hinted that if this man was impressed he may order a commissioned piece right then. I was buzzing with excitement over the possibilities being laid out before me. I was with a wonderful man who adored my son, my talent was being appreciated in new ways (new paying ways at that), and I was no longer living in shadows quietly getting by, and as scared as I was about the unknown, I was just as happy in the here and now.

Chapter Nineteen

Noah

Craig and I were just going over the final plans for the house when my phone rang. Seeing Kiersten's name flash across my screen still pissed me off, but I didn't have quite the same reaction. I was annoyed that she was bothering me – no doubt there – but I didn't hate her anymore. To be honest, I didn't care anymore.

Being with Anna has helped piece back together what Kiersten broke. I was intact with her and getting Roman with her, well that was fucking awesome. He was a cool kid, and I knew one day, when Anna was ready, we would be a family. She was my forever girl. I knew it like I knew my own name.

I just hoped I was doing the right thing when I actually answered the phone this time.

"This is Noah."

"Noah." I could tell I had surprised her by answering.

"What do you need, Kiersten?" Short and clipped was the best I could offer.

"Um, I, ah, okay, sorry, I just didn't think you would pick up." She took a breath before continuing. "Okay, my father has some plans he wants you to look over."

"Why didn't he just call me?"

"Well…"

"Hurry it up Kiersten, I got work to do."

"I didn't tell him we broke up."

"What? It's been months, why not?"

"Well, he just, he really liked you. I didn't want to disappoint him, again." Her voice was thick with emotion. It wasn't for me though. She and her Dad had a tough time, what happened with her and I would not have helped, but there was no way I was going to play along.

"Okay, I get it. But know this when I see him he will know. You think about that before you lie again. So what do you want from me?" I didn't even try to hide my annoyance.

After a lengthy pause, she finally answered. "I need to get these blueprints for a new building to you. Daddy wants you to look them over and decide if you want to be a part of it. Can we get together? For that, I mean."

I didn't like it, but this could be a big project. I wasn't going to throw it away over bitterness towards his daughter.

"Fine. I'll come see you at your office tomorrow."

"Oh, thank you Noah! This means a lot to me and Daddy."

I hung up the phone and shoved it into my pocket. Craig cleared his throat, a question in itself.

"Her Dad has some plans for us to check out. I'm gonna get them tomorrow from her. That's all."

"You want me to go with you?" His concern for me was appreciated, but unnecessary. It was going to be fine.

"No, man, thanks. I don't want to get behind here. You need to be here for the delivery tomorrow. All of the trees and shit are coming."

"Yeah, I forgot about that. Okay, but if you want to skip it, I can go instead." Craig looked like he wanted to say more, but I just shook my head. It wasn't going to be a problem.

We worked out the last details of the house and left the site. Craig was meeting up with Christine later so we had driven separately today. Soon enough he would settle on a house of his own, so our carpooling would come to an end. I can't say I'd miss it. Not having to stop at the apartment will shorten my drive home – I mean my drive to Anna's. Which, to be honest, already felt like home.

I pulled up behind her Jeep and hurried up the stairs. I missed her fiercely today. We were apart too much to suit me and not being able to spend my nights with her was killing me. I understood that it would be hard to explain to Roman, but eventually we needed to do something. This wouldn't work forever.

"Anybody home?" I called from the doorway.

"Shit!" I heard Anna whisper-yell from the kitchen. What was going on? Did I interrupt something? Or maybe there was a visitor she didn't want me to know about? Anger heated through me, unreasonable, but still there. What the fuck was going on? I rounded the corner, ready to beat the shit out of whomever I found, only to see Anna alone, moving around the kitchen like a crazy person.

"Is everything alright?" I asked, a little hesitant. Anna was slamming drawers, tossing boxes, and having what guessed was a complete meltdown.

"NO! Everything is not okay! I just wanted to do something special, and it all went to shit! I am trying to salvage something – anything – and you're already here. Nothing is going the way I wanted it to." With that she burst into tears, covering her face with her hands. I didn't know what was going on, but it didn't matter right now. I moved to her in two steps and wrapped my arms around her. Anna pressed her covered face into my chest and sobbed. I waited until she slowed down a bit before speaking.

"Babe, what's wrong?"

Anna took a few shaky breaths before finally calming down enough to talk. "I got a call from Marco today. He is bringing a hotelier to the meeting – someone who might make a large order right on the spot. I was so excited. And school is starting soon, Roman will be home any minute, and I just wanted to make something special to celebrate all of these big changes. But the cake burned, the chicken didn't thaw, and I have nothing else I can throw together." She got it out in one breath and started crying all over again.

I figured Anna was just overwhelmed and needed a break, so I did what any man would do – I took care of it. "Alright, that's it. You're done."

Anna pulled back as far as I would let her and blinked at me in disbelief a few times. She struggled to get out of my hold, but I held tight. Before she could say anything I explained, "You need a break. You're done, babe. Let me take you and Roman out. We'll just go down to the diner around the corner, no need to dress up or anything. Besides, you look fucking gorgeous how you are right now."

"Ha! I bet I look like hell, you're just being sweet. I think I'll take you up on that though. I am going to clean up a bit first though. Listen for Roman, okay?"

"Yeah, babe, I got him. You go do, well whatever you do, and I'll take care of Roman when he gets here."

Two hours later, after piggy-back rides around the living room and an entire coloring book completed, we were waiting for our food, sipping on milkshakes at the diner. Roman chattered on about his day, only stopping for a few sips here and there. I watched the two of them for a few minutes, soaking in the sight. I wanted this, forever. I knew it in my bones.

Dinner was relaxing, which was exactly what everyone needed. By the time we were done, all of Anna's earlier stress was gone. I wanted to hear more about this new development, but it could wait until Roman was asleep. Well, that, and other things.

It was nine o'clock before Roman was down for the night. It had become routine for me to get him to sleep. It didn't seem to bother Anna, so I was happy to do it.

Anna and I were also developing a routine. I sat on the couch and pulled her down with me. Beers in hand, we curled up together and went over our day. Hearing about Anna's new possibilities made me understand why I found her in the state I did. This was big.

"So, what are you doing tomorrow? What's going on at the site?"

"Oh, there are some landscaping deliveries coming tomorrow. No big deal. I have to go and pick up some plans for a potential job, though, so Craig is going to unload them alone."

"You're looking at a new project? Is it, um, is it around here?" She all but whispered the question, afraid of my answer. She still worried I would leave, one way or another.

"I've worked for the guy before and he usually keeps stuff pretty close to home. But, if it's not, I'll turn it down. I can find work around here. Don't worry about me."

Anna pressed her back into me a little closer, craving contact and reassurance. I was learning her cues, able to anticipate her needs better all the time. I took our bottles and set them on the table in front of us. I wrapped my arms around her and placed a soft kiss on her neck.

"I'm not going anywhere, babe. No matter what, I have no where I want to be more than right here, yeah?"

"Yeah, okay Noah." With that, she turned in my arms and buried her nose in my neck.

We stayed like that for a few minutes. I ran my hand up and down her back, hoping to calm her nerves. I knew I had done my job when she started kissing my jaw and neck. I knifed up from the couch, taking her with me.

I started walking to the bedroom as Anna wrapped her legs around my waist. We fit together perfectly, in and out of the bedroom.

***

On my way up to see Kiersten the next morning, I stopped to see Craig at the site. He was marking the yard for our expected delivery by the time I got there. He spotted me and dropped the can of spray paint before meeting me halfway.

I was feeling uncomfortable about seeing my she-devil ex and the anxiety was coursing through me. Trying to calm down I shoved my hands in my pockets before speaking. "Hey man, just stopped to see if you needed anything from me."

"Nah, Noah, I think it's under control for today. I've got a house to see later today, so I'm taking off after I get the landscaping situated. You ready for this meeting?"

"Yeah, it's nothing. I'm just going to pick the paperwork up and leave. No reason to spend more time there than I need to." I started tilting my head left and right, hoping to relieve some of the building tension. I was not looking forward to this meeting. Kiersten was an unpredictable and conniving bitch, so I had to keep my guard up.

"What did Anna have to say about it? Is she cool with you going to see your ex?"

I hesitated for a damn second, but that was all it took. Craig knew before I could even open my mouth.

"What the fuck dude? You didn't tell her? You are going to regret that, man. When she finds out, and let me tell you they always find out, she will be angry and hurt. You should have told her."

I shrugged at his outburst, "It's not a big deal. Kiersten is gone, over, done. Anna is my future. It's not like I have to work with her, I'm just picking up some damn paperwork."

Even as I spoke the words, I knew it was a lie. I hadn't really thought it through, and by the time I realized my mistake, Anna already knew I had the meeting scheduled. If I said something now it would sound like I was covering. Rock, meet hard place. I was fucked if Anna found out.

"She won't find out. How would she?" I frowned at him, but he threw his hands up in mock surrender.

"Don't look at me, brother. But they always do. You should call Anna and tell her before you go."

"I don't have time. I'll tell her when I get back." Craig shook his head at me. I turned to leave while saying, "It'll be fine." But a sinking feeling in my gut told me I was lying to both of us.

I pulled up in front of the large office building forty-five minutes later. I sucked in a deep breath, steeling myself for the confrontation. Who was I kidding; this wasn't going to be easy. I was still pissed at her. Every time I thought about how she had lain to me, I wanted to hit something. I had never wanted Kiersten the way she wanted me. For me, she was a good time when I needed one; it was never a "forever" thing. Even so, when she told me she was pregnant, I planned on doing the right thing. I was thrilled to be a Dad. I wasn't too excited about having her in my life, but I could have made it work. When I brought over some groceries for her and found her crying, I was at a loss – I figured it was hormones. But as she told me she lost the baby – well I felt nothing. I was empty for a while, then depression set in overnight.

The next day I avoided every phone call. At the time I thought I was being selfish – stuck in my own grief with no care for hers. She made me feel so guilty about that for weeks. Later, when I overheard her telling a friend of hers that it was all a lie, I flipped out. Kiersten hadn't known I was in her kitchen, but when she found the table flipped over, shit tossed everywhere, she knew she was caught. The begging and pleading only enraged me more. I stormed out of the house – leaving behind a few choice words – and never looked back.

As I sat in my truck reliving the last time I saw Kiersten, I could hear my heartbeat in my ears. Rolling my head I heard cracking in my neck – I hoped it relieved some of the pressure I was feeling. It was now that I really regretted not fully divulging what I was doing today. Truthfully, I really hadn't thought about telling Anna. Not because I didn't want her to know, but because I was still lying to myself about my residual rage. I didn't want Kiersten to be able to affect me anymore.

Unfortunately, she still could. With one last deep breath, I opened the door and walked toward what I hoped would be closure.

Kiersten's secretary announced my arrival and motioned me to enter the office. I forced myself to move slowly, with a casualness that I did not feel. When I walked through the door, Kiersten was rising from her chair to greet me. As she stood, her long, blonde hair cascaded down her back and over her shoulders, covering part of the light pink silk top she wore. As she rounded her desk I noticed her tight skirt was showing off more than necessary – probably in anticipation of my visit. I wondered how she even sat down in that thing.

My thoughts were interrupted as Kiersten's arms went to embrace me. I stepped back out of her reach, causing her smile to falter for a second before she recovered.

"Noah, it is so good to see you. I've missed you. How have you been?" Her tone was sincere, but I didn't care anymore. I was here for her father – a man who had helped me build my business.

"I'm fine. Where are the plans? I'm kind of in a hurry." My clipped tone caused her smile to dip even more. Had she expected me to be nice? If she had, she was crazier than I thought.

"Noah, dear," the endearment made me cringe. "I was hoping we could go over them together. Daddy may not be able to aid in this endeavor and wants me up to speed. Won't you sit?"

"Kiersten, what the hell is this? Yesterday, you said I needed to pick up some plans. Now I have to brief you on shit I haven't even seen? No, fuck this. I'll call your father and explain that I am too busy."

Her eyes widened with a mixture of surprise and fear. Her old man would be disappointed – oh fucking well.

"Okay, okay, let me get them. Just give me a minute." I watched her open the drawer of a nearby file cabinet and pull out a large yellow envelope.

"Daddy needs you to complete the blueprints, all the information you should need is in here." She said as she thrust the package into my hands. "So," her voice was quiet and filled with hesitation, "are you seeing anyone?"

"Are you serious?" I was fuming now. I had wanted to find a way to really hurt her ever since I found out the truth about her pregnancy, and I finally knew I could. "You know what? Yeah, I am. I'm seeing a woman that lives near my current project. She's a creative genius, too. Pottery and sculpting, stuff you couldn't dream of doing."

The tears that filled her eyes should have stopped me, but once I got going, I couldn't stop. All the anger I had felt towards her, poured out. "She even has her own business. Unlike you, she didn't have to beg Daddy for a job. I've moved on, Kiersten, so should you."

I watched as her face mirrored her internal chaos. Depression and anger radiated from Kiersten. She hid it as quickly as she could, schooling her features into a blank mask. "I'm happy for you, Noah."

"Me too." With that parting shot, I stormed out of the office to my truck. I had felt justified in her office – now I felt like an asshole. I should have just let it go. But no, I had to be a dick and throw Anna in her face.

I fumed for a few minutes – at myself and at Kiersten. Once I was under control again, I headed home to Anna and Roman.

Chapter Twenty

Anna

It was the first day of school and I was holding it together. The morning went off without a hitch – of course I got nothing done in the studio and woke up early anyway. Roman was excited, and I refused to be upset in front of him – this was his day, not mine. The school bus picked him up right on time, and with a quick hug (or maybe five), my little boy was off.

Back inside, Christine and I started to prep the store for the day. She dusted while I started the computer and pulled out the register drawer from the safe.

"You gonna make it, Banana?"

"Yeah I think so, Chris. The anticipation was worse. He's ready, and I believe I am finally ready."

I finally had my opening for the question I had wanted to ask for a few days.

"So, you guys – you and Craig – you are good now, Chris?" Christine and Craig had started talking to each other again. I was thrilled because they both missed each other so much. It was also good for me since Noah and I were getting more serious all the time.

"We're getting there. We are going to stay friends, for now at least. But not in the same way you kept Noah your friend." She was doing her best to keep a straight face, but her eyes crinkled in humor.

"You just stop worrying about me and Noah. We're doing just fine. In fact, I'm even thinking about letting him spend the night sometime. Of course, that's only if you're okay with that."

Chris just shook her head at me like I was crazy. I guess she was okay with it. We opened the store a few minutes later and were swamped until after lunch. I decided to check the inventory while we had a few moments of peace. Halfway through the plates, the door chimed. I looked up to find a beautiful blonde stunner, in a tight pencil skirt and low-cut blouse, taking her sunglasses off while scanning the space.

"Hi there, can I help you find something?"

"No, thank you. I was asked to drop some things off for Noah Evans. He said his friend could take them for him. Do you know Noah?"

The corners of my mouth started to turn down – his friend? Is that what he told this gorgeous woman I was? And why would he have her drop things off here and not at his site?

"Do you know him?" She asked again, breaking through my internal inquisition. I nodded my head slightly, still confused.

"Yes, I know Noah. He didn't tell me he was having anything delivered here, though, so I'm sorry if I seem a bit surprised."

"Oh, I'm sorry! Noah didn't ask me to bring them here, he just mentioned you at our meeting the other day. I figured it would be nicer for me to bring them here instead of going to a dirty construction site. Is that okay?" I couldn't figure out why this woman made my stomach churn, but something wasn't right.

I started to speak, but Miss Pencil Skirt just kept going. "He never seemed to mind if things were dropped off with me when we were dating, so I just assumed as his friend, you wouldn't mind." Her lips curled up into a toothy grin just as my chest tightened in hurt and anger. He met with an old girlfriend and hadn't told me. Why would he hide that? Unless – no, I wasn't going to go there.

"No, of course, it's fine. I'm so glad to meet you…" I let the words hang, hoping to get her name.

"Kiersten, Kiersten Woods. It's nice to meet you." She held out the papers for me to take and then offered me her hand. We shook hands, our eyes never wavering from each other's.

"Well, Kiersten, you came all this way, have a look around. Maybe you'll find something you like."

She nodded and meandered around while I stewed. I couldn't believe Noah would keep something like this from me. I mean if it wasn't a big deal he would have said something. So the fact that he didn't certainly told me something. My resolve to not be bothered was waning when she dealt the final blow.

"It's been so long since I've seen Noah; it was wonderful to catch up. I've missed him so much. You know, when Noah found out that we lost our precious baby, he was devastated. I am so relieved he has finally been able to pick himself back up and get back to living. He is such a strong man. It really was so good to see him again."

Each word was a dagger in my heart. This woman had been pregnant with his child? He never told me about her. A little voice in my head was reminding me that I hadn't given him the whole story about Henry, but my anger easily shoved that thought away.

"You know," I looked up at Kiersten as she spoke, "I don't believe I need anything else today. I'll see you around."

She didn't wait for my response, not that I would have been able to form words at that point, and breezed out of the door as if she hadn't just set my whole world on fire.

A whimper escaped me when I thought about what her news could really mean. The man had been expecting a child. He was going to have a family. Were Roman and I just replacements for what he had lost? Obviously, Noah and Kiersten were no longer together, but why? Could they not get past losing a baby? My God, was Roman a stand in for him? Did he even really want me?

I didn't see Christine cross the floor to me; my eyes were pooled with unshed tears. I had been completely crushed by this revelation.

"I heard what she said, Anna. I'm so sorry. You need to talk to Noah though. It just seems, I don't know, off. It wasn't a random visit that's for sure." She reached for me as she spoke, but I flinched away at the thought of talking to Noah.

Hugging my arms around my chest I breathed deeply. "No, I don't need to talk to anyone. What I need is to be alone. I'm going into the studio and locking the door. Don't bother me unless it's an emergency."

I handed my phone to my sister and started to walk away. I stopped and added, "Can you tell Noah that I'm just really swamped. Don't mention anything about that woman. I want to think everything through before I talk to him. Okay?"

"Yeah hun, but promise me you will get his side of the story. There has to be a good reason that Noah never mentioned her. Hell, she could be lying for all we know. It has been so long since I have seen you this happy. If there is a way to keep that, I hope you do. So, what do I do with this?" She asked motioning at the envelope Kiersten had left.

"I – I don't know. I guess I'll just put them in his truck tomorrow when he's with Roman. It will be easier than explaining how I got them. I'll see you later, Okay?"

I made my way to the door of my sanctuary, letting my fingertips brush against the picture of Henry and Roman. It was my reminder of happy times and why I keep moving forward.

Locking myself in without a phone wasn't a smart idea since it left me without my playlist. I pulled out a laptop I had stored away and got Pandora up and running. It wouldn't be perfect, but it would be good enough.

I mindlessly moved bricks of clay to my wheel. I began with plates. The monotony of the simple shape lulled me into a blank state. I wasn't relaxed, but I was no longer shaking. It was a small progression, yes, but a step in the right direction. My hands moved by shear muscle memory and before I knew it, my drying shelves were half full. I moved on to vases, hoping the more complicated shaping would remove my ability to think about Noah.

I thought about Craig being so upset with me for not explaining that Henry had died. Did he feel the same way about Noah's past? Knowing Craig, I believed that he probably did. In fact, I would almost bet that he would have told Noah to inform me of the details of his meeting. So I could only wonder why Noah had kept so much from me. I mean, not telling me that his meeting was with an ex-girlfriend, I might be able to overlook. But, an ex that was going to have his baby – a baby he never got to have – I couldn't wrap my head around that. Maybe he wasn't as invested in us as I thought he was.

Two hours had passed when the lamp next to the door flickered. I ignored it, knowing that it wasn't Christine, and since Pete wouldn't bother me if the door was locked, that only left Noah. My heart started to race at the thought of confronting him. I was starting to panic over a conversation we hadn't even had. I was worried he wouldn't take the locked door as a hint; not a minute later my fears were confirmed.

"Anna? Babe, why is the door locked?" Noah's voice came through the door, sounding confused. I had never purposefully kept him (or anyone as far as he knew) out of here. I started to go for the door, but stopped myself just short of the knob. Instead, I took the coward's way out and spoke to him with the barrier still in place.

"I'm busy, Noah. Roman will be home soon and I want to be finished before the bus is here."

"Anna, can you at least let me in? I got done with everything I had planned for the day early. I'd like to just hang out and watch you while we wait for Roman." His voice was muffled slightly by the door, but I could tell he knew something was up.

I wanted to fling the door open and confront him, but I was too afraid that I was right. I was afraid that I was just a rebound and a replacement. "No, Noah. I can't. I need to work. I have to. You can come back tomorrow. Roman will be happy for a break at the park." My thoughts were a jumbled mess and the only way I could get any of them out were in short, specific sentences. I rested my head against the door and wished it was Noah I was leaning on. The emotional void I had achieved was fading fast.

"Um, okay." Noah paused and I could feel his curiosity growing. "Anna, are you alright?"

"Yeah, just – just busy." I lied. I think he knew it to because all he said through the door then was, "Yeah."

No more words went through the wood panel and eventually I heard his footsteps take him away. I walked to a chair and fell into it. The first tear turned into a steady flow and I found myself curled into a ball sobbing. After fifteen minutes I finally got a hold of myself and started force myself to breathe slowly. I regained my composure and readied myself to meet the school bus. I hoped Roman's day had been better than mine.

I learned all about the drama of Kindergarten during dinner. Roman talked non-stop about all of his new friends (not that he remembered any of their names) and his teacher throughout dinner. Apparently this "clipping down" business was serious, so Roman was going to be sure to be on his best behavior for her. As he chattered on, I started to come out of my funk. I had a job to do, the best job, and no one was going to distract me from doing my best – being a good mother would always be my top priority.

It was time to start cleaning up the table and get Roman ready for his bath before he finally brought Noah up. "Hey, Momma, will I get to see Noah as much now that school is here?"

Christine's fork dropped to her plate with a loud clang and I shot her an annoyed look. She picked it up, mouthed 'Sorry' at me, ducked her head, and went back to eating.

"Well, baby, I'm sure it won't be as much, but you'll get to see him." I hoped I wasn't lying. Noah had told Roman that no matter what they would be friends. But was he being truthful? Well, I guess if he was using my son to replace the baby he lost, he would probably still show up. The real questions was, would I, or rather should I, let him? If my assumption was wrong, Noah could possibly be Roman's step-father one day, but if I was right he would be crushed when Noah finally moved on.

I was fighting an internal battle over Noah and Roman's relationship. It was issues like this (well maybe not exactly like this – I mean who would have thought of this) that made me decide that I hadn't wanted to date in the first place. Roman would be devastated if Noah was pulled from his life all of a sudden, but it was a real possibility. I had to talk to someone about this soon. I needed advice from someone I could trust. I needed my Dad.

I finished getting Roman ready for bed and joined Christine in the living room. She had the same expression on her face as when Henry had died and she wanted to console me. This was almost worse. Henry left by accident. Noah, well, Noah had lied to get what he wanted; a ready-made family.

"How are you doing?" My sister moved closer to me and wrapped her arms around my shoulders.

"Honestly? Not very well, Chris." It was all I got out before I started sobbing. It felt like she held me forever while tears streamed down my face. Eventually the well went dry, and I gained control of my breathing.

"I'm sorry, Chris. I didn't mean to just start blubbering." I grabbed a tissue from the coffee table and did my best to sop up the mess on my face.

"Hey, it's what I'm here for. Now, talk to me. What's going on in your head?"

"I don't know, Chris. I mean, you heard her. Why wouldn't he tell me something like that?"

"Anna, I'm going to be honest here, okay? I think he didn't say anything because he doesn't want whatever happened between them to define his life. I have to say, you and…" her face scrunched up and her hand moved dismissively, "Miss Thang, are so different, I have a hard time seeing Noah being serious about her."

"You can see that from a thirty second encounter?"

"Would you have dropped a bomb like that bitch did? Hell no you would not. Therefore, she sucks and you are fucking fantastic. I know and Noah sure as hell knows that's the truth. Got it?"

I couldn't help but laugh at her logic. Nor could I argue against it – it seemed pretty solid to me.

Christine looked up at me through her long, dark lashes. "So, are you going to call him?"

"No. Not yet." She started to say something, but I cut her off. "We can talk tomorrow. He planned on taking Roman to the park, so I'll just explain that I need some time to think. I won't keep him from Roman, for now."

"Time to think? Are you sure, Anna? Maybe you need to just face this head on. I'm sure if the two of you talk, it can be worked out."

"I don't know, I guess. But I still want a day to think it over. Maybe I'll talk to him tomorrow night. A real conversation, I swear."

Christine seemed to be content with that answer and nodded to the television. I just forced a smile and let her turn it on, hoping that whatever ridiculous show she chose would distract me.

Chapter Twenty-One

Noah

Something was going on with Anna. I didn't know what the fuck it was, but it was obvious. She didn't even open the studio door to see me yesterday, and it was more than a simple slab of wood was separating us. When we first started seeing each other, Anna always tried to keep me at arm's length, and just when I finally got those arms wrapped around me, she pulled away again. I needed to stop this shit before it went too far.

Craig and I finished up for the day early so we could view a house he was interested in. He wanted my opinion on some of the things that would need to be fixed before he put in an offer. Driving behind him I thought about Anna. I would make sure I stayed for dinner tonight. She wouldn't be able to avoid talking to me. I just hoped I could handle what she had to say.

Craig pulled up in front of an older colonial and stopped. I parked behind him and stepped out onto the pavement. "So this is it huh?" I asked, noting the crumbling walkway and exterior in desperate need of attention. Easy enough fixes, but they can help keep the price down when negotiating since most people can't look past that.

"Yeah, it needs help out here, but what I really want is your opinion regarding the floors on the second floor. I think I can work with them, but you have a lot more experience." He pulled a key out of his pocket and walked up to the front door.

I looked around, my perusal is careful to make sure he hadn't missed any expensive issues out here. Walking into the house, I noted that the layout was more open than I expected, given its age. There must have been a remodel done some time ago, and based on the fixtures, I guessed the late eighties, early nineties.

Craig and I made our way to the second level in silence. He pointed out the rooms and let me take a tour by myself. I left him at the top of the stairs and focused on the floor. Well, I tried to. Thoughts of Anna ate at me. The longer it took to find out what was going on, the worse it got. I shook my head, trying to focus on the house. After thirty minutes I rejoined Craig, and we headed out.

"So, do you think they are solid?" Craig asked when we got to the street.

"Yeah, there are some loose boards, and some weak spots, but they're strong and solid. We may need to replace a board or two, but I don't think the cost will be outrageous. Are you thinking this is the place?"

"Yeah, I really think so. If I can get it for the right price, I think this will be a good place to start a life."

I chuckled at him. Who would have thought that after everywhere we've been that he was just starting his life at thirty-two? In a way I understood him though. I knew that a whole new life started for me when I met Anna. I'm guessing that was the life he was looking forward to starting – one with roots, structure, and a family.

"So, have you heard any more from Kiersten?"

Surprised, I turned to Craig. "Why would I hear from her? It was her father's project."

"Man, that woman is nuts. I wouldn't be surprised if she made the project up just to see you." He shook his head in disgust. "What did Anna say when you told her about it?"

It was an innocent question – one I should have had an answer to. I should have said something to Anna right away, but the longer I took – well fuck it I was acting like a pussy and I knew it. I just didn't see why I should piss her off for no reason.

When I didn't answer right away, Craig smacked his hand against the back of his truck, shocking me back to reality, "What the fuck man? You know what? Whatever, I don't care what you do, but you are going to fuck everything up with her. You should have told her." He moved towards his door and ripped it open before I could say anything. Craig twisted his neck and held my eye, "You're gonna regret it, brother. Fuck, you already should."

With that my best friend jumped in his truck and sped off. I was left alone with my thoughts – and they were a fucking mess. I knew why it bothered Craig so much. His ex had done a number on him awhile back. She never really lied, but shit, the crap she kept from him was fucked up. She was the reason he had a hard time trusting anyone now. He was right though; I should have said something – anything – about seeing an old girlfriend. I know I sure as shit would have wanted to know. Hell, I would have wanted to go with Anna if she was going to a meeting with an ex. But, being bullheaded I chose to not give Anna that option and now that could come back to bite me.

I got in my truck and headed to Anna's place. Roman would be home from school and waiting for me by now and fuck if I didn't miss him. Being dismissed by Anna yesterday meant I didn't get a chance to see him – or her – and that wasn't happening today.

I pulled up in front of the store and grabbed the new football I bought for Roman. He had put in more effort than any five year should and I wanted to reward him. It was something my Dad would have done for me. I knew it could be risky, but I had let myself think about life without Anna or Roman and the image scared the shit out of me. I wanted them both forever. Hell, I wanted to add to our family too. I had thought Anna was feeling it too, but I wasn't so sure now.

I was determined to find out what was going on after Roman went to bed tonight. But first, we had some serious park time to get to.

I tugged the door open and walked in to the store, scanning for Anna. I didn't see her anywhere, but did spot Christine with a customer. I nodded to her and walked through the back to the office – which I found empty. Confused, I turned towards the studio, but the light was off.

I pushed through the doors and waited for Christine to finish. It wasn't like Anna to not be here, and even though I didn't think I needed to know where she was all the time – nope, that wasn't true, I did need to know. She was mine and if I didn't know where she was, how could I get to her if she needed me?

"She's with Marco, Noah." Christine's voice broke into my thoughts. "They had a meeting set up, but he called and moved it up. He said he wanted to talk to her privately before he introduced the other buyer to her."

"Oh." That was all I could say. Two days ago Anna would have called me right after hearing from Marco, so why hadn't she? What the hell happened?

"I guess it was pretty last minute, huh? Well, I'll wait outside for Roman, okay?"

"Sure, Noah. Just have him bring his stuff in here. I'll bring it up later for him." She gave me a sad smile and turned away.

"Christine," she looked back at me over her shoulder, "Are you alright? I mean, you seem upset about something is all. You can talk to me, too, you know?" God, these women made me such a pussy.

She smiled, "I know, thanks. I'm fine, I'm just – just," her shoulders slumped, and she inhaled a shaky breath, "I just want everything to work out for my sister. I want her to be happy."

With that she busied herself with papers and I took that as my cue to leave. I sat on the tailgate for twenty minutes, trying to answer emails and calling in last minute orders while I waited for Roman. The whole time I was trying to get work done, my mind was on Anna. I don't know what Christine had meant, but I wanted Anna to be happy too. I would not let her pull away from me without a fight.

Roman jumped off of the bus and waved goodbye through the door. The driver eyed me, but when Roman launched himself into my arms and started chattering non-stop about his day, she smiled and shut the bus's door while rolling away.

After getting Roman's school stuff situated, I pulled the new football out of the bed of my truck. Roman was ecstatic and within seconds threw it in the air. I eventually got him to calm down enough to get his stuff put away and back outside. Roman then proceeded to pull my arm the entire time we walked to the park in an attempt to get me to go faster.

Twenty minutes into our football practice, Roman was ready to just run around and be goofy. Before I let him go to blow off steam, I needed to pick his brain. "I missed you last night buddy. Sorry I wasn't around. Did you and your Momma do alright without me?"

"Yeah, Momma said with school starting and stuff you might not be around as much. It's okay. We ate dinner, but it's more fun with you."

I schooled my features, so I didn't upset Roman, but inside I was on fire. Why the hell did Anna tell him I would be around less? Shit, I thought we were moving closer to me being around more. Hell, I wanted to be around them all the time.

"Rome, it might be tough some days, but I'll make sure we still hangout, no worries, OK?"

"Cool." His grin hit me hard, right in the chest. Roman and Anna were my life, and right then and there I knew that I was going to marry that woman. No matter what was going on in her head, we would deal with it together.

"She was sad."

What? I jerked my head at Roman's declaration. "What do you mean bud?"

"Momma, she was sad. She tried to pretend she was happy, but I know."

"Why was she sad?" I prayed he knew, but knowing Anna, she kept it inside.

"I dunno, but she looked at me funny a lot. And Aunt Chris cleaned up dinner. That only happens when Momma's sad."

"Tell you what. I'll talk to your Momma tonight, okay? We'll see if I can fix it."

Roman was happy with that answer and darted back out to the slides. I watched him for another ten minutes before letting him know it was time to go. School had been tough on my boy – and yes he was my boy – so I carried him piggyback the whole way, even up the stairs to the apartment.

Opening the door I heard Anna's voice. She sounded tired and upset. When we came around the corner she snapped her mouth shut before pressing her finger to her lips to Roman.

"I gotta go, Mom. Roman and Noah are back. Yeah, just tell Daddy I called and want to talk to him soon." She paused, listening to her mother, and I swear I saw tears pooling in her gorgeous eyes. "Love you too. Bye."

Anna set the phone down and slipped a plastic smile onto her face. I stared at her in disbelief, but her expression never wavered. Instead, she turned and started fussing around the kitchen asking Roman about his day. I watched her silently; neither of us had said a word to each other. She didn't approach me in any way – in fact she was staying as far away from me as she could without being obvious to Roman.

The door clicked shut, and I turned to see Christine. Her eyes widened for a split second before she caught herself. "Hey there, Noah. Anna, I'm just going to change really fast and then I'm going out." I nodded to her as she walked by. The door to her room shut as I turned back to Anna.

I noticed Roman sneaking glances between me and Anna, his face showing more than a little concern. I wanted to ease his mind – and mine – so I walked to Anna and slid my arms around her waist from behind.

I felt her stiffen at our contact and I swear my heart stopped. The same woman who would press herself into my mouth as I made her come, was now closing down at the slightest touch. Ignoring all of the thoughts racing through my head, I pushed for conversation. "Chris said you met with Marco today. How'd that go?"

"It – it was good, I think." She moved from my arms to place a bowl in the sink and stayed a foot away from me. I wasn't going to let this happen, so I wrapped my hand around her wrist and gave her a gentle tug, pressing her against my chest. Her breathing hitched, her way of protesting without words.

Instead of asking about the meeting – which would have been safe – I dipped down and placed my mouth next to her ear. "Babe, talk to me. What is going on?" I said it in a whisper, just for her, and she started to shake her head vigorously.

"N-n-nothing. I'm just distracted by all of this new stuff." She lied. I knew it and she knew that I did, but with Roman here it wasn't the time to get into it.

Moving back, I rested my forehead against hers. I breathed in her scent and forced myself to calm down.

"Okay, babe, we'll talk later." I squeezed her hips and walked away, never looking at her eyes. I think it may have killed me if I had.

Dinner was awkward and filled with tension. Roman felt it too and didn't argue about bedtime. Again he asked for me, and again I was more than happy to oblige. At least someone there wanted me around.

With Roman asleep, I figured we could get everything hashed out. I needed to tell Anna about Kiersten, but first I needed to find out what was going on with her. But before I could say anything, she was moving towards the door.

"Noah, I'm sorry. It's been a hectic day. I just want to take a hot shower and go to bed."

What. The. Fuck. She dismissed me, again. "Anna, are you alright? You've barely said two words to me, you don't want me to touch you, hell you didn't say anything about your meeting with Marco today. What's going on?"

"I told you, I'm tired." The words snapped at me like whips. She wouldn't even talk to me and it was pissing me off.

"You know what. Forget it. Fine. You're tired. We'll deal with it tomorrow." I grabbed the doorknob and yanked it open. I wanted to turn around and shake the shit out of her and force her to tell me, but I knew better. I flew down the stairs and out the back door, letting the night air cool me off. I walked around the building to my truck and hopped in. I gripped the steering wheel tightly and rolled my shoulders. The stress was eating me alive. As I started the engine something caught my eye.

There was an envelope on the passenger seat. Confused, I picked it up and pulled out the contents. Shit, fuck, and damn were all the words I could think of. It was paperwork for the new build and Kiersten's business card was stapled to the top of it. How the hell had this gotten in my truck? As soon as my brain made the connection between the envelope and Anna's sudden change in demeanor, I threw the stack of papers to the floorboard and flung the truck door open. I'm not even sure I shut it before racing back to Anna's apartment.

I took the stairs two at a time and started pounding on the door. At this point, I didn't care if I woke Roman up. I had to get to her. "Anna! Open the door!" I listened for a second and slammed my hand against the door again. "Anna!"

Anna cracked the door open, but I pushed my way in. I saw her head drop as she closed it behind me. I glared at Anna, pissed at myself for letting it get this far and hurt that she did not want to fight for me enough to even ask about Kiersten.

"Did you put something in my truck, Anna?"

She sighed before answering. "Yes. It was delivered to the store."

"Babe, where did that envelope come from?" I hoped to hell she would say by courier, but I knew there was no way I'd be that lucky.

"A woman brought it by yesterday." She barely spoke above a whisper, but I could still hear the pain in her voice.

"Is that why you were locked away? Why you wouldn't even look at me?"

She nodded, her eyes glued to the floor. I hated seeing her like this. Moving closer, I cupped her face with gentle hands and pulled her chin up, forcing her to meet my eyes. "Shit, knowing her, I can only imagine what she said, and I can almost guarantee it wasn't exactly truthful."

"So you didn't have a meeting with your ex-girlfriend and not tell me about it?"

I cringed, "No, I did, but I was going to tell you, I swear. I should have said something about meeting with my ex, but at the time, I just wanted to get it over with. I'm sorry. Okay?"

A tear slid down her cheek and I brushed it away with my thumb. There were so many emotions surging through her I couldn't get a handle on what she was thinking. "Is that all you were going to tell me about? That the meeting was with your ex-girlfriend?"

I should have thought a little longer before answering. I should have known that a bitch like Kiersten would want to stake a claim on what she thought was hers. But I didn't do any of that. Instead, I just reacted. "What else would I need to tell you?"

She closed her eyes and pulled out of my hands. As Anna walked away from me and sat on the couch, I realized what she already knew. "Noah, you can't be that stupid." Anna finally lifted her eyes to me, but the icy glare that hit me made my knees buckle. "She told me about your baby. And I started to think, maybe, just maybe, this," she motioned her hand between us, "this isn't what I thought it was. Maybe you are just trying to find a replacement for what you lost."

To say I was stunned would be a hell of an understatement. I couldn't even speak. At no point did I ever think Anna would feel that way. How could she think that? "Anna, don't say that, don't even think it, you and Roman are everything to me. Are you sure Kiersten told you everything?" It was hard to talk about the lies and betrayal, but I had to get through it. "Anna, Kiersten lied, okay? To me, to you, to everyone. There was no baby."

That got her attention. Anna searched my eyes, and when she found the truth, I could see some of the tension leave her body. "Kiersten was never pregnant. She just told me she was so I would stay with her. I met her though her father, a man that had originally helped me start my business by giving a young kid a break. When Craig and I bought a house to flip close to her, we started dating. It wasn't anything serious, just some fun. You need to believe me, I never had any thoughts of keeping Kiersten in my life and I thought we were on the same page. The job I was working on was complete and Craig and I were heading here and I said goodbye to her. Two days after we spoke she calls me up and tells me she took a test and we were going to have a baby.

"I dropped everything when she told me I would be a Dad. I wasn't real happy about who the mother of my child was, but I wasn't going to hold that against my kid. I tried to stick it out, but I knew, once the pregnancy was over, I was done with her romantically. I even thought about fighting for full custody once my baby was born, but she wasn't a drug addict and her family had the money to fight back. After a couple weeks, Kiersten told me she lost our baby. It was the worst pain I had ever felt. I'm tellin' you Anna, I thought I would die right there. I felt bad for her, too, and wanted to help her through her grief, so I didn't leave right away."

I reached out and grabbed Anna's hand, needing something solid, something real, to ground me. I could feel anger pulsing from me, but I couldn't stop it without her touch. When she didn't pull away, I continued. "I was in her house one day, I guess she didn't hear me come in, and overheard her on the phone with someone. She was explaining how she had lied about being pregnant, hoping that I would stop using condoms and get her knocked up for real. I left and never wanted to look back. Craig took me out that night and got me shitfaced. Other than a heated argument when I confronted her, I haven't had anything to do with that woman. I don't want anything to do with anyone but you got it?"

She gave me a weak smile as another tear escaped. I had hoped it meant she understood that I wanted her for her. I loved her. Shit, I loved her and never told her. I couldn't tell her now, it would be tainted. I didn't want her thinking that I would throw those words at her just to keep her. I needed Anna to know that I meant them. So I kept them to myself and regretted it immediately.

"I'm sorry, Noah. That was horrible of her. But, I still need some time to think."

"No, you don't!" I exploded, making her jump halfway across the couch. I felt like a complete asshole for scaring her. Lowering my voice, I all but begged her, "No, babe, you need to talk to me. Let's get it out there so we can fix it, yeah?"

Anna pressed her lips together and shook her head. "No, Noah. We need some time apart. I understand that there was no baby, but at one point you thought there was. It was cruel of her, and I wish it had never happened. But I need you to give us some space. What if..." her voice broke. I started to say something, but she shook her head, her eyes pleading with me to hear her out. "What if your mind latched on to Roman as a way of coping? And I know you're attracted to me, but what if your deeper feelings are false? I need to know, and you do too, whether or not this is real. Please, just give me that, alright? Just a small break to evaluate everything. Can you do that for me?"

I didn't want to. I wanted to pick her up and carry her to the bed and show her how I felt. I'd fuck her until she couldn't think straight and then make love to her until she felt how much I loved her all the way to her bones. But I also wanted to show her I respected her and ignoring her need for time wasn't going to prove that. I forced myself to nod. Grabbing her hands, I placed a kiss on one and then the other, lingering slightly to inhale her scent one more time.

"What about Roman?" My throat was so dry I could barely get the words out. I was afraid she would keep me from him, but it was her right. Anna always did what she thought was best for her son, and this situation would be no different.

"It would break his heart if I forbid him to see you. I don't want to do that to either of you. But, Noah, you can't be around as much, not until we get this figured out. That way, if you and I can't get past it, it won't be as hard on him when you are gone."

Gone. The word pierced my heart. I lifted my eyes to Anna's and saw the same pain I felt reflected in them. As much as I wanted to grab her shoulders and yell that I wasn't going to go anywhere, I restrained myself. Neither of us wanted this, but I understood why she was asking me to back off. I had never thought of her or Roman as replacements, but thinking it through, I could see how someone might get that idea. Anna was barely holding it together, and I didn't want to cause her any more pain, so I started for the door.

Before I shut it, I turned and asked, "Why didn't you just give me the envelope?"

Anna gave a cheerless laugh. "I hoped you wouldn't see it until you got home. I wasn't sure I could handle the conversation we just had." She gave me a sad smile.

"Babe, you are so much stronger than you think you are." I shut the door and made my way to my truck. Not knowing how much beer we had on hand, I stopped at the store before making my way to my apartment. I needed something to get through this, and I couldn't have what I wanted most – Anna.

Chapter Twenty-Two

Anna

I got through the next few days, but it was difficult. The pain I felt from separating myself from Noah was almost unbearable. Even though he had only been a part of my life for a few months, I saw him everywhere I looked. The couch reminded me of how it felt to have his arms wrapped around me watching a movie. The bed, well, the bed was obvious – I was definitely ruined for other men. Hell, the Keurig coffee maker almost made me cry thinking of how nice it was to have Noah make us coffee to sip on as we caught up after a long day. Whispers of doubt flittered in and out of my head. The most prominent thought was: if it hurts so much to be without him, should I be?

Roman could feel the tension between us when Noah picked him up and dropped him off; I could tell he was nervous about what it might mean. I knew he was just as attached to Noah as I was. I had done nothing to protect his pure little heart and now he would have to face the consequences of my thoughtlessness.

Noah kept his word and gave me space. He tried not to stay too long and kept putting off dinner when Roman would invite him. I should have appreciated what he was doing, but it made me even more depressed. Part of me wanted Noah to put up more of a fight. I was thinking like a teenager – wanting him to respect my wishes and fight for me at the same time.

I recognized that I was going to have to start limiting, and possibly eliminating, the time Noah and Roman spent together. Noah and I were apart, and I couldn't see letting Roman spend more time with him. If I felt that I couldn't trust him with me, I sure as hell shouldn't trust him with my son. The biggest hurdle I had was convincing myself that I didn't – all I knew for sure was that I was head over heels in love with him.

That evening I invited Noah up for dinner, prefacing the invite with the "we need to talk" speech. I could see the torrent of emotions in Noah's eyes, but he just nodded and headed out with Roman, promising we would talk after he was asleep. I flittered around everywhere trying to ease the nervous energy pulsing through me. Mixing bowls and pans littered the countertop while the sink was filled with other odds and ends. As I pulled everything out of the sink and filled it with hot water, I went over what I needed to do again. I had to make the break as clean as possible for all of us. Mixed signals would only lead to heartache. Mine I could deal with, but Roman's would be devastating.

I had a huge dinner done and ready before they came home. I had gone all-out with pure comfort food. Even if preparing the fried chicken, mashed potatoes, green beans, cornbread, and brownies didn't calm my nerves, I would definitely eat away the sadness I would succumb to after Noah left. I had been alone in the apartment this whole time. Christine was more than understanding when I asked her to go to Pete's for dinner tonight. I hated kicking her out of her own home, but there was no way we could have an audience for this.

Noah and Roman got home later than they normally did, in fact it was almost completely dark, which told me Noah realized this may be the last time he got to spend with Roman. The idea that he thought to make the memory last a little bit longer made me falter and want to nix my plan and just move forward. But right as I was ready to say "Fuck it" and let him kiss away the ache in my chest, that perfect face and body belonging to Noah's ex would pop up and my insecurities would take over. I couldn't let go of the fact that he never told me about her and what she had done. I also couldn't get past him not telling me that she was the person he was meeting. Why would he want to hide that? He said he thought it didn't matter, but if I had been meeting an ex – if I had one living – he would want me to tell him.

I agreed with Craig about keeping secrets. Noah had, and it left us staring at each other from across a deep chasm – one I couldn't find a way across. I was broken, again. But this time it wasn't an accident. Noah had left things out purposefully, not lied per se, but definitely omitted important details.

Dinner was a quiet affair, Roman tried to fill the tension-filled air with stories about school and what he and Noah had done at the park, but even he grew quiet after some time. His small face pointed at his plate, eyes sliding back and forth between Noah and me. He knew something was coming, but he didn't know what it was or how bad it would be. Noah on the other hand did seem to be able read the writing on the wall. Every so often he would reach over and squeeze Roman on the shoulder in a comforting manner and smile.

I made it through dinner and bath time, but when it was time for Roman to go to bed Noah grabbed my hand and turned me to face him. "Please, Anna, let me." I swear his voice cracked a little, and I found my head nodding before I even had time to decide. It was only right to let them have a goodbye.

I tidied up the spotless living room, trying to keep busy while I waited for Noah to emerge from the bedroom. I was adjusting a pillow when two massive, warm hands clamped down on my waist. I straightened quickly, only to have Noah place his soft lips at my ear. The warmth of his breath made me want to sink back into him. "Don't do this, Anna. Please, don't push me away." Noah's voice was pleading, his grip tightening as if he would not let me go. Part of me didn't want him to ever let me go, but I couldn't listen to that part tonight. I needed to remove Noah from my life – at least for a little while – so I could think. I couldn't think about anything but letting him wrap his strong arms around me when he was around.

"Noah," I sighed, turning around to face him. His hands released me only enough to let me turn, clamping down as soon as we were face to face. "I need a break. From you, from us, from all of it."

"A break won't fix anything. You need to talk to me." Noah's voice was rough with emotion. He was losing control, and he didn't like it. "I'm sorry I didn't tell you I was meeting with her, okay? I didn't think about how it could affect you. It won't happen again."

"You're right, it won't. It can't. I can't do this Noah. Roman –."

"Roman nothing! Roman is fine, he's upset because you're upset, but if you would just listen, just believe me, you wouldn't be upset either." Noah pulled himself up to his full height and stepped back without releasing me. He was breathing hard now, his voice rising slightly with each word.

"I have listened to you. I have heard how sorry you are about the meeting. What I don't hear is you understanding how deeply you not telling me about Kiersten and your relationship cut me. To be caught off-guard, in my own store, and told how you lost your child with her, how devastated you were, how do you think I felt, Noah?" I was seething, clenching my jaw as I spoke. My voice rose with each word, anger outweighing sadness.

He opened his mouth to speak, but clamped it shut when I continued. "I'll tell you since you don't seem interested enough to ask. It was humiliating. I was being sized up – and torn down – by a woman I didn't even know existed. She made sure I knew that you had been with her, and she damn well could tell that it was news to me. And do you know what the worst part was? When she told me about the baby, my heart broke. But it broke for you! It killed me that you had to endure that. True or not, I know it wounded you."

"I'm so sorry she ambushed you. I realize I should have told you. You gotta know seeing you like this, upset and cold, it's killing me to live with the fact that I did this." The emotion surged from Noah's eyes as if his very soul was reaching out to touch me.

I momentarily rested my hands on his, slowly peeling them away from me. Taking a step back I cut into him a little deeper, "You need to stay away from me and Roman. I can't have you around him right now. I don't know if I can get over this, and it isn't fair to string both of you along."

I regarded him carefully – his hands fisted by his sides, his jaw ticking in anger, his eyebrows forming an irritated V above his eyes. Then, as quickly as it started, he relaxed. "Okay, Anna. I understand. But please remember, I'm a phone call away. If you or Roman needs me, I'm here." He closed in on me, taking my hands in his with a firm, but gentle grip. "You. Are. Mine." He punctuated each word with a soft kiss to my forehead. The mixture of domineering and sweet confused me. "I will prove to you that we belong together, Anna. I swear it. I will give you some space, but I will not disappear. I cannot see a life without the two of you and I am willing to fight for it."

My traitorous heart leapt at his words. I wanted to climb up his body and latch on to him. Before I could give in to the temptation, Noah asked for one last favor. "Make sure he knows it has nothing to do with him, yeah?"

"I will. I don't want him mad at you, and I don't want him mad at himself. I'll take the blame, don't worry." Tears pooled in my eyes. Trust Noah to put Roman ahead of us. Trust Noah. I want to do just that, but fear had a way of taking over my entire being. Until I could get over being afraid I couldn't truly trust him.

"I don't like that either, babe. I don't want him to be mad at you. He needs you."

I tried to swallow, but it felt like my throat was closing. I just nodded silently. Noah wrapped his arms around me, hugging me tightly. I would miss this so much. I couldn't help but return the embrace, tears stinging the backs of my eyes. Noah kissed the top of my head before lowering his lips to my ears. "One phone call. Shit, just text the word 'now' and I'm here. Take some time, but don't give up, yeah?"

I couldn't respond. My head and my heart were at war. I just closed my eyes and inhaled his scent deeply, not wanting to forget it. Noah let me go and walked away. The coldness seeped into my body as I watched him. As the door closed the dam finally broke and tears streamed down my face. I curled up on the couch and waited for Christine to come home. I needed my sister.

By the time my sister walked through the door, I was done crying, but I was still on the couch, knees tucked under me, hugging a pillow.

Christine and I talked about everything that happened. She understood my concern, but still believed that Noah truly cared about me.

"That man loves you. I'd bet on it."

"Then why not tell me? Why would he want to hold something like that back?"

Christine just raised one brow at me like I was an idiot; which I was. It wasn't like I was proclaiming my feelings to him – how could I expect to get exactly what I wasn't willing to give?

***

Roman asked constantly about Noah the first week he of our "separation". The next week he only asked a few times, and those questions were him wondering if Noah was upset over something he had done. Each inquiry made my heart break all over again, for me and for Roman.

Noah was perfect for both of us, I knew this. But I couldn't get that bitch out of my head. Pete thought I was being stupid. He didn't say it, but I could tell – he was my brother so I had memorized his different faces over the years. He and Noah had become friends, and my brother wasn't going to pick sides. That wasn't in him and I would never ask him to. He was kind about it, though, and didn't mention Noah to me. Actually, everyone was very careful not to talk about Noah, at least not in front of me. But it didn't take a genius to know what they were talking about when I would walk into a room and the conversation immediately stopped.

Every once in a while Noah would walk by the store on his way to Pete's and wave through the window and I had to restrain from running out onto the sidewalk and tackling him. He had yet to catch me staring because I was quick to look away. This incensed my sister more than anything.

"Why can't you just give him another chance? You are being so stupid!" She yelled at me one day before storming out the back door.

Even my parents were walking on eggshells. I could tell my Mom wanted to say something, but she held back. My Dad had made a couple comments about wishing there wasn't so much extra food at family dinners, but I ignored them.

I refused to let them sway me. In other words, I was being stubborn. And it was killing me. I ached for Noah, I missed everything about him. I was lonely, and for the first time since I lost Henry, it really bothered me. I had finally gotten a taste of something real and what did I do? I ran at the first sign of danger.

Christine was taking a break from paperwork, helping me restock shelves mid-day when her resolve broke and she brought him up. "Anna, how long are you going to do this to yourself? To Noah? Hell, to Roman? Look at you. You have bags under your eyes from not sleeping. And don't think you're fooling me – I can hear you crying at night."

I stared at her in shock. I had seen the looks she gave me in the morning, but I hadn't realized where they stemmed from. I just thought it was because I looked like shit.

"I just don't know, Chris." I said as I worked on the shelves. "I just wish I knew what was going on in his head."

"Well, the only way you're going to know anything is if you talk to him! I can tell you that man misses you. The way he looks at you when you're looking everywhere but at him is heartbreaking. Noah loves you."

"Don't put words in his mouth. He has never said that."

"I don't care, Anna. It's true."

"I'm going to head into the office for a while. I need to place a few orders." I was evading. Christine realized it, but thankfully she didn't call me on it. I kept myself busy the rest of the day. I didn't want to keep rehashing the same things with my sister.

Roman came home from school while I was on the phone with a supplier. He walked past the office and up the stairs without as much as a nod in my direction. I hung up as quickly as I could and hurried up to him.

I found him lying on his bed, staring at the wall. It was a heavy mood for a kindergartener. Slowly, I sat next to him and placed a gentle hand on his side. When he finally turned to me my heart stopped at the sight of unshed tears in his perfect brown eyes.

"Roman, what happened? You can tell me anything, you know?"

"These boys were teasin' me 'bout being little. Said I was lyin' about playin' football with Noah." The sadness in his voice almost undid me. I wondered how much of it was about the teasing and how much was related to Noah's absence.

"Rome, I'm sorry those kids were jerks. I'd like to tell you that it's no big deal, but I know it is. You just need to know that some people are just unhappy and they want other people to be unhappy too. Know this, though, you are an awesome kid, and you're a lot like your Daddy." My voice started to falter at the mention of Henry. Roman turned to face me, awe etched in his features.

It was times like this one I wished Henry was around for Roman. Tears pricked the back of my eyes, but I blinked them back, needing to be strong for my son. I gave him a little squeeze and continued. "When we were little, your Uncle Pete would give your Daddy the hardest time about being small. The whole time he was growing up your Daddy was bitty. At one point even I was taller than he was. But you know what?" Roman's eyes bore into mine, waiting for me to go on. "Well, about the time we got to high school, he started growing and didn't stop until he was danged near done with college. Your Daddy ended up a few inches over six feet tall – taller than Uncle Pete." Roman's eyes got wide and then he started to giggle.

"Did Daddy make fun of Unca Pete then?"

"No, baby, your Daddy remembered how it felt to be teased about things he couldn't control. He did his very best to not put people down. That is something I truly loved about him." I cleared the emotion from my throat.

"He was cool. Everybody says so. He'd prol'y know what to say to those kids next time they bug me."

"Just do your best to ignore them. If that doesn't work, tell someone. Try not to be hateful like them, but if you don't see another way, I'll never get mad at you for defending yourself." I wrapped him up in my arms. "Feel better?"

"Well, kinda. But…" Roman's head went down, hiding his face from me. I could barely make out the mumbled words, but caught Noah's name.

"What did you say, Rome?"

"I asked if I could call Noah and ask him for something to say to them." His little voice was so hopeful I almost gave in, but I didn't. Instead, I chickened out.

"Rome, he's busy working. Maybe later, okay?"

I watched his mood go from sad, to relieved, to angry in a matter of minutes. Without a word he shrugged out of my hold and grabbed his crayons and a pad of paper. He lay on his stomach on the floor and started to draw, completely ignoring me. I wanted to be angry with him for his attitude, but I knew it was my fault. I had not only brought Noah into his life, but I have effectively forced him out of it too.

A few hours later I was being eaten alive with guilt. I made my way back into Roman's room. He needed a man to talk to, and lucky for us, I knew one that would never turn him away.

"Hey, Roman." He looked up from his toys for a second and then went back to playing. Apparently he was still mad. "I was thinking, maybe Uncle Peter could give you some advice about these bullies. We can call him right now and ask. What do you think?"

"Ok, but you hafta leave the room. It's guy talk."

I handed him my phone, holding back a laugh, and nodded my approval. I shut the door to give them privacy.

Chapter Twenty-Three

Noah

I was with Craig at Pete's house when Pete's phone rang. I couldn't help but listen in when I heard that it was Roman on the other end of the line. A hundred different thoughts hit me at once. Was something wrong? Was he hurt? He wouldn't be calling if he was hurt. Shit, was Anna hurt? Why didn't she call me? I was lost in a building wave of emotion when Pete shoved his phone in front of my face.

"My nephew needs to talk to you, man."

I ripped the phone from his hand and pressed it to my ear. "Roman, are you okay buddy?"

"Kinda." His voice was quiet as if he was unsure of how to talk to me. It killed me that he had lost faith in me – in how I felt about him. But it was my fault, so I pushed passed it.

"Well, your uncle says you need to talk to me, something wrong?"

After a deep breath, Roman went into detail about some shitty kids at school – kids I would need to have a conversation with. I gave him a few quick comebacks he could remember and told him how cool I thought he was. I even offered to come to school and show everyone how good he had gotten at catching a football. He shied away from that, but I wasn't surprised – Roman isn't the type of kid to seek attention.

"Hey, Noah?"

"Yeah, bud?"

"Well, um, could you um, could you not tell Momma that I talked to you?" The words rushed out of him like a train. I hated that he felt that we weren't even supposed to talk to each other.

I took a deep breath and released it. "Bud, I'm not gonna lie to your Momma. But I'll tell you what. I won't bring it up. But, if she asks me if I've spoken to you, I have to tell her. Deal?'

He was quiet, mulling over what I said. After a full minute of silence he finally agreed.

"Okay Rome. Look, you learned your numbers, right?"

"Yes! I'm good at writin' 'em now."

"Good, that's good. Here's what I'm gonna do. I'm going to give you my phone number, you write down all the numbers I give you and if you need to talk, you just punch them into the phone. I'll always answer. What do you say?"

"Cool."

Damn right it was cool.

***

I couldn't think straight. I missed my woman something fierce. I had stopped myself a few times from hauling myself over to her place and spanking her perfect ass for severing herself from me. And Roman, damn I missed that boy. His fucking smile could charm candy from a baby, I swear. I stayed away physically, but kept up with her life through Pete. He was a good brother. He never told me too much, just enough to know that she wasn't having an easy time without me. I hated that she was hurting, but damn it, it was her own fault. At least, that's what I told myself. Craig just shook his head when I would say that, making it clear he did not agree. I didn't either, but hell, it wasn't entirely my fault. Just, you know, mostly.

The past few weeks had been filled by a sick pattern. Wake up, work, eat, and sleep – the entire time my mind was on Anna. I couldn't even escape thoughts of her in my sleep. Shit, the dreams I were having were in-fucking-sane. As much as it killed me to wake up, I wanted to take notes for when I finally got my woman back. With everything my subconscious was thinking up, we would need an entire weekend away to get reacquainted.

Craig had made an offer and bought the house he showed me. We had been discussing the renovations on the porch when he brought up the job Kiersten's father had offered us. "I'm glad you turned that bitch down, brother. We're going to need a job close to home, so I can get some time in on my place too."

I shook my head at him, snorting. "I didn't even talk to her. I called her father and told him we didn't want to venture too far away this time. I explained that we had both found a place that we wanted to settle down and he understood. No big deal."

We were overlooking the plans Craig had drawn up when an older man walked up to us. I had seen him before, but it took me a minute to place him as Craig's neighbor. "You fellas going to fix up this old place?" His accent was thick, and judging by his voice, he still smoked three packs a day.

"Yes, sir. I bought it a couple of weeks ago. We're going to bring it back to life." Craig was beaming – do men even do that?

"Well, I heard something like that. Thought I'd ask for myself. You boys any good at fixin' houses?"

"Come on up here and sit awhile. You're welcome to take a survey what we're planning here. You want a cup of coffee? We've got plenty, and it's getting pretty cold out here." I was hoping the guy was here to offer work and it sure as hell wasn't below me to be hospitable.

"Don't mind if I do, son." The old man took his time up the steps and took a seat next to Craig. They started going over the plans as I went inside to grab the coffee. It didn't take long, but by the time I got back, they were already talking about what needed to be done at the neighbor's house.

"Noah will be happy to have some work here in town, too." I heard Craig say, making me pause. I waited for him to continue, but I couldn't make out what he was saying.

"Got woman problems, does he, eh?" I decided it was time to make myself part of the conversation.

"I've got coffee for you," I said as I pushed the screen door open. I put it down on the table in front of him, and offered my hand, "I forgot to introduce myself, I'm Noah Evans, sir. And you are?"

"Randall Pryor, nice to meet you." He replied, shaking my hand with a firm grip.

I leaned back against the porch railing and took a sip from my mug, settling in for what I guessed would be a long conversation. Older people seemed to be able to go on for a while, and judging by the empty driveway at Randall's house, he didn't have anywhere to be.

"So, who is she?" Randall gave me a knowing look, even when I tried to act confused.

Caving, I all but mumbled the answer, "Anna Johnston, you know her?"

He nodded, "Knew her grandfather. Watched Malcolm grow up and have his family right here in Franklin. Nice family. You sure know how to pick 'em." He gave me a toothy grin before continuing, "What did you do?"

"Me? Why do you think I did something?"

"He didn't tell her he was going to meet with his ex about a job opportunity." I wanted to punch Craig right in his big-ass mouth.

Randall started laughing so hard – and then wheezing – I thought we would have to call an ambulance, but he got himself together before standing upright again. Then he looked me in the eye, an intense expression on his face. "Go to her. Don't give up, not even for a second. You want her, you go get her." The conviction in his voice was telling. This man had been in my position and knew how important making the right decision was.

Chapter Twenty-four

Anna

I spent a few hours in the studio this morning since there was a ton of bisque ware that needed to be glazed and put in the kiln. I loved bringing my pieces to life with color, but even this wasn't helping lift the mood I was in. When the kiln was full, I double checked the settings and my timer before cleaning up after myself. With everything complete, I made my way to the store to relieve Christine.

"Hey, I'm done back there for a while. If you want to catch up on your paperwork before I call Marco back, you're more than welcome."

"I don't really want to stare at a million pages of numbers right now. You go ahead and take care of that phone call. Maybe we'll have something to celebrate tonight."

"If you're sure..."

My sister waved me off, and I headed back. I sorted through the portfolio I had shown Marco at our initial meeting, picking up the notes I had made. My fingers trembled as I dialed his number, still nervous about the entire venture. I forced myself to breathe and calm myself as I listened to the phone ring.

"Marco Rinaldi speaking."

"Marco, it's Anna Johnston returning your call."

"Anna! Wonderful, wonderful. I have spoken with my client and he is eager to meet you and discuss exactly what he is looking for. However, he is only in town for a few days. Will you be able to join us tomorrow afternoon, around two-thirty?"

I would need to find someone to take care of Roman, but the short notice was good since I had less time to psych myself out.

"I'll make it work. Where would you like to meet?"

We decided on a small restaurant in Charleston that Marco often used for meetings of this nature. I made sure he agreed with my selection of pictures in my portfolio one more time before we said our goodbyes. I was nervous to say the least, but still felt prepared. Hopefully confidence would come soon.

I pushed the doors open and called out to my sister, "I need you to be here for Roman tomorrow, I'll be in Charleston at a meeting."

"I can't, hun, I'm meeting with the CPA, remember?"

"Oh crap, I forgot. What am I going to do now?"

The door chimed as Christine said, "Maybe Pete can help?"

"Maybe I can help with what?" I looked up to see Pete walking in – with Noah.

"Yeah, what do you need help with?" The familiar deep voice vibrated through me, waking me melt just a little.

"Oh, it's nothing. I just need Pete to get Roman after school tomorrow." My eyes flicked back and forth from my brother to Noah.

My brain was at war with my pride; I wanted to peek at, no stare at, Noah, but I didn't want to give in either.

"I can do it." Noah replied before Pete could. I looked to my siblings for help, but they refused to meet my eyes. I knew what they were doing, and I didn't like being forced into doing things, but I didn't have a choice. I took a deep breath and made myself finally look him in his perfect blue eyes.

"That would be really helpful, Noah. Thank you." I couldn't help but return the full smile he gave me. It felt too good to hold back. Noah moved closer to me, his eyes locked on mine.

"Anything for you, babe. Anything." He placed his hand on my hip as he spoke, but pulled it back to his side in the same moment. I at once missed the warmth of his touch and leaned forward towards it, causing me to stumble slightly. The movement caught his attention, but thankfully Noah didn't say anything.

Pete on the other hand, did not let it pass. "You alright there, Anna? Drinking this early in the day?" I narrowed my eyes at him, but he just cackled at me and talked to Christine. I turned my attention back to Noah while butterflies moved with ferocity in my stomach.

"I have a meeting in Charleston, so I'm not sure what time I'll get back. Can you take care of dinner for him?"

"You bet. I'll even make sure he eats something healthy." Noah winked at me with a slight grin. God, I missed this. But I was still so unsure of everything and I couldn't force myself past it.

Roman came home moments later, threw his bag on the floor, and launched himself into Noah's arms. "Noah! What are you doing here? Are you taking me somewhere?" Roman's eyes were shining with hope as he waiting for the answer.

"No, buddy, I'm just stopping by. But maybe we can hang out tomorrow, yeah?" Noah rested his forehead against Roman's before setting him down. I wondered why Noah was vague about watching him tomorrow, but I just told myself he wanted it to be a surprise. I could go along with that. It was such a touching moment between the two of them and it caused my throat to tighten and I had to fight back a few tears.

It was then I knew that I was ready to sit down with Noah and put everything I was feeling out there and see what happened. Maybe everyone was right; maybe we just needed to talk it out. Or, more likely, maybe I just needed to put on my big-girl panties and get over it. At this point I wanted to kick "maybe's" annoying butt. I hated being without Noah more than I hated how learning about his past from an ex-girlfriend made me feel. As soon as I got through this meeting I needed to decide once and for all; no more waffling.

Chapter Twenty-five

Noah

Thank fucking Christ for Pete. He had given me a bullshit story that he needed to get something from Christine. So, naturally, we had to stop by the store before heading to Fritz's, and we could not have had better timing. Now I get the chance to be her fucking knight in shining armor. I jumped at the opportunity to not only come to her rescue, but also spend time with Roman, no questions asked. It wasn't until later I realized that I didn't ask what the meeting was for or who it was with.

By the time Pete and I got to Fritz's I was grinning like a damn fool. I flagged down a waitress, and we got our orders in.

"So, I don't have to tell you to not fuck this up right?" Pete growled at me. As if I needed him to tell me this was fucking huge.

"Nah, man, I know it. It was divine intervention that had me in there tonight, I cannot blow this opportunity."

"I'm glad to hear it, Noah. I'm straddling a wide fence right now, and as much as I should not tell you this, being her brother and all, you need to know."

I leaned in, not wanting to miss what he had to say. Pete's been good about keeping me in the know without breaking the "brother code." He mentioned that she's not as happy as she was, and that Roman was having a hard time with my sudden disappearance. I hated that for both of them, but, selfishly, I was happy too. It was good to know that they missed me because I missed the hell out of them. Everything around me reminded me of both of them, and it was slowly killing me.

"Anna, shit bro, Anna is going downhill fast. It's the worst I have ever seen her." He gave me a pointed look. I took a second to catch on to exactly what he was saying, but it finally hit me. It was worse than when Henry died. Is it wrong that I wanted to jump up and start yelling? Probably, but right now I didn't care. It was the sign I had been waiting for since I found out what really happened to him. I couldn't hold back my cocky grin to save my damn life.

"Don't make me punch you in your mouth, dude, that's my sister, and he was my friend. I'm just saying that she is walking around like a zombie unless Roman is around. I can't watch her go through it again. You gotta fucking fix this." Pete's thick finger jabbed at me with each word.

My face fell as his words sunk in. I looked him in the eye and promised, "I will fix it. I can't keep going on like this either. Every day is a new type of torture. I swear to God, Peter, I'm going to make her happy again."

Satisfied with my reply, Pete made sure I knew he was free if I needed him to take Roman tomorrow if things went really well. Since we were talking about his sister he didn't want to say anymore, not that he needed to, and we dropped the subject.

It worked out well because Craig finally showed up. He grabbed a beer from the bar and made his way to our table. "Noah, that guy, Randall, he has a back porch he wants turned into a sunroom. We've got work, brother." He clapped me on the back as he greeted Pete.

The rest of the evening was focused on blowing off steam from our week. Pete had not only turned out to be a great friend, but he was an excellent find regarding work. Craig and I decided that he was going to be our go-to for plumbing on all future jobs. Everything was falling together now that Craig, and I had found a place to settle down. I was beyond thrilled that one town had offered us both that place. We had been working together for so long that now I didn't think we would be able to do it without each other.

Yup, I was going to make the most out of tomorrow. At this point I would beg, borrow, or steal my way back into Anna's arms.

Chapter Twenty-six

Anna

It had rained all day, but I refused to let it put a damper on my mood. Bad weather made for a slow day, and with Christine gone, it was quiet. I kept myself busy and distracted by cleaning. The entire store was gleaming by one-thirty when I could finally close the store without feeling guilty.

Gathering my things quickly, I sprinted out of the back door and to my Jeep, slamming the door behind me. I threw my hood back and started the engine. Well, I tried to, but the damn thing wouldn't turn over. After a few tries I dropped my head to the steering wheel, not caring that the horn was blaring.

Tears pooled in my eyes at the thought of missing my meeting, and I couldn't think of anyone to call. I was staring through the windshield at the downpour when a shadow appeared with a knock at my window. I jumped back in shock before Noah's face came into focus. The sight of him drenched was something dreams were made of. The long sleeve shirt he was wearing allowed the rain to mold the fabric to every hill and valley his muscles created. I couldn't help but stare, only coming out of my daze when I noticed his lips moving.

Noah opened the door slightly, shielding me from the rain with his body the best that he could. I looked up into his eyes and saw that they were filled with concern. "Jesus Anna, are you alright?"

"Y-y-yes, I'm ok." I shook my head, remembering why I was sitting there. "No, actually, I'm not. I can't get it started."

"Jesus Anna, you scared the shit out of me. C'mon." Noah pulled me out of the Jeep and leaned in to grab my things. I was ushered to Noah's truck, which was parked right behind me, and seated before I realized what was going on. Noah was on his phone, walking in the rain towards the driver's side.

"Thanks, man. I owe you one." He said in to the phone as he pulled from the curb. "I'm going to take you, Anna. We'll figure out what's wrong with the Jeep tomorrow."

"What about Roman? Who will get him?"

He waved his phone at me before tossing it in the cup holder. "That was Pete. I called him and asked if he could help us out. It's covered."

My body sagged in relief at his words until I realized that we would be in such close quarters for a length of time. To avoid conversation I grabbed my portfolio and started flipping through pages, doing my best to ignore the overwhelming desire to reach over and thread my fingers with his.

Out of the corner of my eye, I watched Noah strip his shirt off and reach in the back for a fresh one. I snuck a quick peak of his perfect torso before darting my eyes forward again. I heard him laugh softly, so I slid my eyes to the side only to glimpse him smirking at the windshield. I guessed that he caught me, but I didn't acknowledge him. Noah knew I was avoiding him and wasn't going to pressure me – his kindness chipped away at the wall I had put between us.

We were just outside of Franklin when the hard rain turned into a torrential downpour. I wasn't sure how Noah could even see the hood of his truck, but he kept going. Too nervous to stay idle, I pulled out my portfolio and went over my notes, preparing myself. It wasn't until the truck was almost stopped before I realized something was wrong. Looking up through the windshield, my heart stopped. The bridge was covered in rushing water. How in the world was I supposed to get to Charleston now?

"Give me a minute, there is another way. We'll figure something out, Anna." Noah's voice was almost reassuring, but I knew the truth.

"Noah, the only other way will add almost an hour of backtracking to the trip. There's nothing we can do, I'm going to miss the meeting." I took a few deep breaths, trying to gain some composure before continuing. "I will call Marco and see if we can reschedule. His buyer won't be in town for a while, but surely he'll still be interested."

Noah gave me a small smile before he checked his phone, most likely looking for new directions. I scrolled my contacts list and stared at Marco's name. I was too scared to call – the thought that I was losing a rare opportunity was eating away at me.

Before I could hold it back, a sob escaped me, causing Noah to jerk his head up at me, his face a mix of concern and sympathy. My shoulders sagged under the pressure, giving in to the feeling of defeat. I started to press the call button when my phone became blurry with unshed tears.

"C'mere, you." Noah's deep voice filled me with more comfort than I had the guts to tell him. I blinked away the tears and shifted to find his arms stretched out, waiting to hold me. It was so tempting and I was so upset, I moved closer to him, letting his strong arms wrap around me. The heat from his body warmed me to my core, soothing and calming me. Noah always knew what I needed, and he just held me in silence.

It was this moment that I realized what I was missing most in my life; him. The thought scared me though because after everything I had found out I wasn't confident in our relationship. I was so confused. One minute I felt like I needed time for Noah and me to build back up what Kiersten had ripped to shreds and the next I wanted to let Noah tie me to his bed and fuck the bad memories away – and I knew he could do just that.

I looked up into his dazzling blue eyes and gave a weak smile, trying to assure him. My body wanted more though, and before I realized it I was leaning toward him, my eyes focused now on his mouth. My tongue instinctively darted out to wet my lips, causing Noah to do the same. I watched his Adam's apple bob up and down as he swallowed in anticipation. Noah's arms tightened around me, bringing me firmly against him, closer to my destination.

Before I did something I couldn't take back, my phone chimed loudly, breaking the spell. As I moved to answer it my attention shifted to Noah, his mouth opened as if he wanted to say something, and then snapped shut, jaw clenching. We cleared our throats in unison as I saw Marco's name flash across my screen. I opened the message quickly and almost choked on my relief.

"It's Marco. They need the meeting to be pushed back two hours. They still want to see me today, but they ran into delays. Oh, oh, Noah, this is perfect!" I flung my arms around him, overwhelmed at the good luck.

Keeping a tight hold on me, Noah replied, "That's great news, babe. Let's get turned around and moving. I'll get you there." He smiled at me, but it didn't quite reach his eyes. Instead, they seemed disappointed. I knew exactly how he felt – any other time I would have probably said to hell with the consequences and mauled him right there on the side of the road, but I couldn't miss this meeting.

I released him and leaned back against my seat, directing Noah to a different route to Charleston. I wanted to reach over and grab onto his hand, but the sting of learning about Noah's past – one he did not share with me himself – held me back. I needed to let go and trust him again before I could allow myself to go running back into his arms. I just wasn't sure I could do that.

I knew Roman would have wanted Noah back in our lives. He had dealt with the loss of Noah as I had expected. He had finally stopped asking about him, and just as he was getting the chance to spend some time with him, Mother Nature ruins the plan. Maybe that was for the best. If I couldn't let Noah back in, it was best that they stay apart. I wasn't sure what hurt more, knowing that I was single-handedly breaking Roman's heart, or that I was doing it to myself as well.

Chapter Twenty-seven

Noah

If that fucker Marco wasn't so important to Anna, I would break his fucking neck for his shitty timing. She was right there! Anna was going to kiss me, letting us get back to being us, and what happens? Her damn phone goes off! I have got to do something to get her to see the truth and get her back to that place where we were about to become a real family. All I see is her. All I want is to be with her and Roman. No matter what, they are mine – and I wasn't going to let bullshit from an overeager ex take them away.

I took a risk and looked over at her as she called Marco back, confirming the time change. I continued to steal quick glances at her even after she hung up with him, barely restraining myself from hauling her over next to me. Anna finally hung up and focused on the passing scenery – what little she could see. The rain had let up just enough that driving was no longer half-way impossible, but it still came down in sheets all around us.

I noticed her wringing her hands while she stared out the window, and a part of me couldn't help but hope it had something to do with me. The thought had guilt churning my stomach though. This moment was about her – I should be encouraging her, not hoping to get her under me. But right now, all I can think about was her hot little body writhing as I – shit! My pants started to tighten at the thought of her, forcing me to try to adjust how I was sitting. Thankfully, Anna doesn't seem to notice.

Twenty very quiet minutes later, Anna finally broke the silence. "Thank you for, um, helping me I mean." The words come out in a soft whisper, and since she didn't turn from the window, I almost missed it.

"You don't need to thank me, babe. It's what I'm here for. I'd do anything for you, you have to know that." If I am going to prove myself to her I couldn't hold back anymore. I had to convince her that I was all in and not going anywhere. I knew it wasn't the time to have that conversation, but it would be soon.

I reached over and took a firm hold of her hand. Surprised, she finally took her eyes off of the rain spattered window and looked at me. Her eyes were sad, but she didn't pull away. I gave her hand a squeeze and then let go. I wanted her to stay in control of how fast we moved forward, but as soon as she would give me the smallest sign that I had the go ahead, all bets were off and I would claim her – body, mind, and heart – all of her.

My mind went back to imagining her naked, and my cock started to grow – again. Just the thought of her had me as hard as steel. I shifted again in my seat and this time Anna noticed my discomfort.

"Everything okay?" Anna asked.

Is everything okay? No, it's not okay. I want to go back to holding you in my arms, feeling your need for me pulsing from your body. I want to kiss you until I make you forget your own name. I only thought this, still in control enough to not divulge my carnal thoughts, pushing her farther away. I twisted towards her and realized she was still waiting for an answer.

"Yeah, babe, I'm just anxious for this to happen for you. I want you to get what you've worked so hard for. I want everything for you." I wanted to hold her eyes, but I was still driving in a fucking crazy-ass storm that would not let up, so I had to shift my eyes between her and the road ahead.

I may not have been able to see her entire reaction, but I definitely heard the sharp intake of breath that told me she understood – and was surprised – by my conviction. We sank into a comfortable silence for the rest of the drive, both lost in thought but still aware of each other.

Anna guided me to the restaurant where they were meeting, using her cell phone's GPS when she became unsure. When we reached our destination, I pulled the truck into a parking spot close to the front door. As I opened my door, I noticed that Anna didn't move. She was either just used to me getting her door, or she was scared shitless. I moved quickly out and around the truck to her door and opened it. Anna still didn't move when I extended my hand, so I cleared my throat.

Her brown eyes blinked a few times before she turned to me and smiled, placing her hand in mine and threading her warm fingers through mine. What I wouldn't do to see that smile every fucking day, I do not know. I help her out and watch her gather her things. As she walked towards the restaurant doors, I placed my hand possessively on the small of her back guiding her towards her future – a future I was determined to be a part of.

***

I walked Anna to the hostess, looking for a place to watch her from. I wanted to be available if she needed me, but didn't want to intrude on her big break. When Anna pointed Marco out to the hostess, I noticed he was alone. Since the buyer wasn't there yet, I followed Anna to the table.

Marco rose from his seat to greet Anna, eyes sliding to me in question. "Noah Evans," I said extending my hand in greeting. "I've heard a lot about you, Marco."

Marco stood at my gesture and smiled genuinely, "As I have about you, Noah. It's nice to finally meet you." I was surprised that Anna had mentioned me, but I tried to not let it show. Anna had always said Marco was very professional towards her, but it was nice to see for myself that he had no romantic intensions toward my woman.

Spotting the bar, I pulled Anna to me as she went to sit. "I'll be right over there, okay? If you need me, just let me know."

Anna was surprised. "You're not staying?"

"Babe, I know you don't need me. You've got this. I'll be close, don't worry, but I know that you don't need me to hold your hand here. They weren't expecting me, so it might make you look, I don't know… weak, if you bring someone as "back up" that is." I jerked my head toward Marco, "This guy knows how talented you are, but this other one might need convincing. Now, blow his fucking mind." Without thinking, I kissed the top of her hand and took a step back. She gave me a real smile, squeezed my hand, and took her seat.

I found a spot at the bar that gave me the best view and settled in. I ordered a beer and some food to keep me occupied, then turned to check on Anna. The other man had appeared in the time it took me to get comfortable, and the waitress was taking an order from him.

I made small talk with the bartender, shifting my attention between him and Anna. Her face was so expressive; I knew exactly what was going on without having to hear a word.

They spoke animatedly, pointing at pictures and gesturing to each other with over-the-top hand motions. She was in her groove, feeling good about everything being discussed. I didn't feel like Anna was going to need me, so I turned my attention to the bartender. The restaurant was pretty quiet, and all he had done for the last ten minutes was wipe down glasses – we both needed a distraction.

We were in the middle of discussing how to fix the flooring in his bathroom when something behind me caught his attention. With the flick of his eyes, I turned, wondering what he was warning me about. As soon as I saw Anna's beet-red face, I knew I missed something important.

"Man, I don't know what he just said, but she seems pretty embarrassed."

"I think I'm going to go join them, thanks for the company."

I stood up and caught Marco's eye. This was his last chance to stop me from coming over. Not only did he not stop me, he looked thankful. I did not like that at all and hauled ass to the table. As I got closer, Anna's face became a mixture of fear and relief – it didn't look good for the suit at this point. I placed my left hand on the back of Anna's chair – a clear statement – and offered my right to her buyer.

"Sorry I'm late, babe. Please, introduce me." This was still her meeting, but I hoped to hell she would give me what I wanted – needed – to hear.

"Mr. James, this is my fiancé, Noah." Anna's smile lit up the room, while her words lit me on fire.

I hid my surprise from Mr. James, but I think my fucking heart stopped. Fiancé – that sounds fucking perfect. I shook the man's hand, eyeing him closely. He was pushing forty, at least, relatively good looking with a deep tan and manicured hands. His brown hair was glued in place – in other words he looked like a pretty-boy pussy.

"Nice to meet you, Mr. James. Again, I'm sorry I was late. Traffic was ridiculous. You would think some people had never seen rain." I gave him a toothy grin while gripping his hand tightly. He tried to squeeze back, but I think his jaw was clenched tighter than his hand.

"The pleasure is mine, please call me Richard." He bit out.

After I made my point, I took the chair across from my woman and called the waitress over to order a beer. The three of them discussed an order over the next twenty minutes before Dick (I decided it suited him better than Richard) decided it was time to go and excused himself. He promised to be in touch with Anna soon though.

Watching him walk away, my curiosity finally got the best of me. I cleared my throat, getting both Marco's and Anna's attention. Marco just smiled and shook his head at me while Anna tried to figure out what to say.

"So, what happened? He said something to you, I could tell by your reaction from all the way over there, hell the bartender could."

"Um, he, uh, well…" Anna focused on her plate, shredding the roll while trying to think of something.

"Come on, Marco?"

"No! I'll tell you. Sheesh, he just wanted me to visit the lobby of one of the hotels." She looked up at me with half a smile before rushing out, "And… after that, to have dinner with him. He wouldn't let it go at first."

I wasn't surprised, really. You'd have to be dead to not see how gorgeous my woman was, so I could forgive him hitting on her, this time. Anna expected me to blow up, I could tell, and if I had been at the table at the time – fuck, she wouldn't have sold him a damn thing.

"Ok, that would be awkward." I said with as much nonchalance as I could muster.

Anna looked up from the now-destroyed bread in complete shock.

"Shit, Anna, you're beautiful, of course he would ask you out. Good thing for him that he dropped it when I got here though. Now," I leaned forward and stared right into her eyes, "when did we get engaged?"

"Oh!" She immediately burst out in laughter. "I just thought 'boyfriend' sounded so, I don't know, young. I know you hate it, and I didn't want to say 'my man' so it just fit. That's all." Again her eyes went down.

"Sounds logical to me." I knew she wanted me to drop this, so I was willing to let it go – for now, "So, are we celebrating?"

Marco finally spoke up at that point, "Oh yes, Noah, absolutely. This was very productive."

Chapter Twenty-eight

Anna

I was finishing up in my studio when Christine opened the door and walked in without warning. Judging by the look on her face, she was somewhere between wary and out-right scared.

"Chris," I drew out her name, "what's going on?"

I watched my sister turn around and quietly shut the door. Christine took tentative steps towards me – my anxiety increasing with each one.

"Anna, I think you should sit down."

I stood there frozen. My thoughts went to Hell right away. "What's wrong with Roman?" I croaked the words out, fear constricting my throat.

"Nothing! God, sorry, nothing is wrong with Roman." She had the decency to be ashamed.

"What the hell, Chris?! You better spit out whatever is happening right now. You scared the shit out of me!"

"Okay, okay, I'm sorry. Nothing is wrong with Roman, but what I need to ask you *does* have to do with him. He asked me something, and I wasn't sure how to answer."

Relieved but wary, I moved to the counter, bracing myself against it. I couldn't imagine what Roman had asked. We were far from, um, "reproductive" discussions so that wasn't it.

"What could he have asked that has you in such a tizzy?"

"He, um, he," she hesitated before continuing in rapid fire, "He wanted to know if I thought you might let him put a picture of Noah on his nightstand too."

I had not been prepared for that. I knew Roman had become attached to Noah, and I had all but eradicated their time together since the "Kiersten incident." The change was met with resistance from both of my guys – not that Noah was mine.

It had been a couple weeks since I told Richard that Noah was my fiancé and Noah hadn't brought it up once. I was grateful that he didn't press the issue. I was struggling with feelings regarding my relationship with Noah. I kept going over the same thing – he was amazing, but what else do I not know about him? My trust in him had been shattered therefore I was uncomfortable with his and Roman's relationship continuing. I felt that they needed to continue to stay apart while I sorted everything out.

I wanted to ask why he would want a picture, but the answer was obvious. Noah was incredible with Roman. He treated my son as if he was his own flesh and blood. If I was honest with myself – something I wasn't quite prepared to be – I would admit that Noah treated both of us as if we were his family.

"You should let him, Banana. You and Noah belong together, and eventually you two will find your way back to each other. There is no reason to not give this small thing to Rome."

"I don't know, Sis. I appreciate your faith, and I do miss being with him. It's just hard to get the thought out of my head that we are just filling a hole."

"Anna, Anna, Anna. You are! Hear me out." She gave me a look that kept me quiet, but I shot daggers at her with my eyes. "You two are what *make* him whole, don't you get it?! Even if the crap with his ex had never happened, he was yours from day one. And he is so good with Roman. It's time to move past this, hun."

She gave my shoulder a light squeeze, leaving me to my thoughts. She was right – I knew it. I just had to figure out how to get past myself and embrace life with Noah.

When I left the studio a short time later to get back to work behind the register, I felt light-headed. I figured it was stress, and pressed forward, dragging my hand across the wall of the hallway as I walked. By lunchtime I was a spinning mess. Christine came out of the office to ask me what I wanted to eat, only to press her cool hand against my forehead and send me upstairs to bed refusing any argument. The climb was difficult, but I managed with only a few pauses.

I was too exhausted to even attempt to take my clothes off, so I just laid myself down and wrapped the blanket around me. I was asleep within minutes.

***

I stirred at the sound of Roman and Christine in the kitchen, but I couldn't move out of my bed. I knew my sister would take care of him, so I let sleep take me again.

I woke up again and the whole place was quiet. The rest helped me gain some strength, so I forced myself out of bed to see what was going on. Stumbling to the kitchen, I spotted a note on the counter by my teapot. I figured Christine took Roman out to give me that time to sleep, but when I saw the note was from Noah, I was shocked.

Anna -

I took Christine and Roman out for dinner so you could rest.

We'll bring back something for you too.

If you need me, I'm there. Just call.

Noah

It was hard to not feel tingly all over. Not only did Noah plan on bringing me dinner because I was sick, he took care of Roman and Christine too. He truly cared about us – all of us – as if we were his family. I made a cup of tea and headed back to my room to sleep. Visions of time spent with Noah flashed before me as I finally allowed myself to let go of my inhibitions and fall.

***

"Anna, babe, you gotta eat something." Noah's whisper pulled me from my fever-induced sleep.

I opened my eyes to see him bent over me, eyes filled with concern. "Noah. Hey." It was all I could get out, my throat was dry and my entire body weak.

"Hey, yourself. I brought you some soup from Rinaldi's. Kathryn said it would fix you right up. Wouldn't even let me pay for it when I told her you were sick." Noah slid his hand under me, helping me up to a sitting position, and eventually helping me to stand.

"I'll come eat a bowl since you went to all that trouble. Thanks for coming over," I leaned my full weight against his solid body – partly from the fever, and partly because I had missed being this close to him.

I peeked in on Roman, who was playing quietly in his room. He looked up and gave me a big smile. "You feel better, Momma?"

"Not yet, baby, but I will soon. You need to be good for Aunt Christine tonight, okay?"

Roman's lips quirked in confusion, "Auntie Chris left, Momma."

I looked to Noah in bewilderment. Where was my sister? She would never leave me alone like this. At least Noah was here, he would be able to get Roman to sleep – Roman prefered that anyway.

"She got a phone call and had to leave in a big hurry. Don't worry, I'll stick around and get Little Man to bed. Now, c'mon, you need something to eat."

I let him lead me to the table and then watched as he got my dinner together. His back was to me, and even in my hazy state, I was able to appreciate the view. Every time he stretched, his shirt rode up, giving tempting glimpses of his seductively formed torso. Noah's jeans hugged his perfect ass as if they were made just for him– a fact I couldn't help but be thankful for.

Noah sat with me as I ate, talking about his day and relaying everything Roman had informed him of his day at school. He explained that he had told Roman to steer clear of me tonight because he didn't want Roman to get sick or cause me to over-exert myself.

When I finished, Noah gave me some medicine and helped me back to my room where I tried to crawl back into bed, before Noah stopped me. He gently removed my clothes, dressed me in much more comfortable yoga pants and a tank, before tucking me in with care. His soft, cool lips pressed against my forehead with tenderness as I closed my eyes.

"I will stay on the couch tonight, okay?"

"You don't have to do that, Noah. We'll be fine."

"I know I don't have to, but it would make me feel better knowing I was here if you needed me. Roman complained about being achy at dinner, and if he ends up sick, you won't be able to do much in this condition."

He was right, I felt terrible, and I was able to admit to myself that it felt good to have him so close. If I would have had any sense, I would have offered to share the bed, but at this point, I was lucky to still be awake. I nodded weakly to Noah before pulling the pillow tight and falling back asleep.

Chapter Twenty-nine

Noah

After making sure Anna was asleep, I went to Roman's room to start getting him ready for bed. He chattered on the entire time about everything from school, to Teenage Mutant Ninja Turtles while I found some shorts and a tee for him to wear.

Anna had asked that I stop taking him to the park so often, giving me some bullshit excuses about school, so I was glad to get a little extra time with him. I really thought we were moving past everything the day we rode to Charleston, but Anna just continued to keep me at a distance. As much as I hated to see her sick, I hoped that this opportunity would help sway her.

After getting Roman to sleep, I grabbed a blanket out of the closet and got as comfortable as I could on the couch. I laid there for a while, fighting with myself over slipping into Anna's bed, but eventually the logical side of me won, and I stayed put.

Crying woke me up a few hours later. I bolted upright and ran for Roman's room. As soon as I walked through the doorway, the stench of vomit hit me. I pulled the now-soaked blanket and sheet from Roman's bed right away, then put a hand on his forehead, only to find that he was burning up.

Ripping his puke-covered shirt off his tiny body, I debated on what to do. Anna wasn't in any shape to deal with this, so there wasn't a point in waking her. I scooped him up and with my free hand, grabbed fresh clothes from his drawer. Roman was crying, but he was still calm enough that I could do what needed to be done with minimal effort. As I moved his limbs I spoke softly to him, telling him that he would be fine and I was going to take care of him.

Once I had him changed, I found Anna's cell phone and scrolled through her contacts until I saw "Mom" and hit dial. Without a doubt she could help. It took a few rings – it was close to midnight – before someone finally picked up.

"Anna, what's wrong?" I was surprised to hear Mitchell answer.

"It's Noah, Mitch, Anna's pretty damn sick, so I stayed to take care of Roman. She took some medicine, and she is out, I don't think she could wake up for this if she wanted to."

"Wake up for what? Where's Christine? You know what, never mind, it doesn't matter. I'm just getting my head together. Ok, what's going on?"

"Well, Roman started throwing up, and he is hot as hell, and honestly, I was hoping for some help. I'm still really new at all of this."

"Alright, I've been here before, here's what you need to do. Take his temperature; there should be a thermometer in the bathroom. If it's over 103, I'll give Pete a call. He's closer to Anna than we are, so he'll be there before she needs anyone. You are going to take our boy to the hospital. Rose and I will meet you there to make sure he has someone they'll let stay with him. With our luck, Rose will have worked with one of the nurses on duty and we won't have any trouble."

I followed his instructions as he gave them with Roman in my arms – his body a raging furnace against me. I took his temperature and my stomach rolled, "Malcolm, it's 104, I gotta take him, now."

"Go, son, I'll get Pete over there, so don't worry about Anna. He'll get her there as soon as he can wake her up."

"Alright, I'm leaving now." I ended the call and carried Roman into Anna's room so I could put her phone by her. I wanted to make sure she could get in touch with me quickly.

"Noah, I don't feel good. I want my Momma." Roman's voice was weak and his body was shaking so badly I was having a hard time holding him.

"I know, Buddy, but your Momma's sick too. I gave her some medicine that made her sleepy. I'm gonna take care of you, okay?"

He turned slightly in my arms to look at me, his eyes were glassy and his face was bright red. "Okay." He laid his little head against my chest and I almost started crying. There was nothing in this world I wanted more than to get my boy better.

Finally in his coat, I got to my truck as fast as I could. I knew Anna would be pissed, but I folded the console back and placed Roman next to me, letting him lean against me the entire way to the hospital. I hated that I couldn't hold him because the truck was a stick-shift. I needed a new fucking truck.

When we got to the ER, Roman was drifting in and out of consciousness. I was careful to get his head in the crook of my arm and carried him in. Thankfully, Malcolm and Rose were already there and had informed one of the nurses of our arrival. Rose knew a couple of the nurses on duty and convinced them I needed to stay with Roman until Anna could get here.

Roman's entire body emitted so much heat it was as if he was on fire as we were ushered into a small, sterile room. Hospitals had never bothered me before, but the smell of disinfectant was about the make me lose my shit. I hated that he had to be here and somehow felt like it was my fault. I should have known he was going to be sick – he had been complaining about pain earlier. Anna was in no shape to be responsible, so I should have given him something. Guilt ate at me and I clutched Roman tighter.

"Noah," Rose placed a hand on my arm, "they need to do their job, honey."

I blinked at her, not understanding what she meant. A slow smile spread across her face as she leaned over, whispering in my ear, "They are so lucky to have you." Her hand squeezed my tense arm as she stepped back. "Noah, you have to put him down." She removed her hand and motioned to the paper-covered exam table.

I stood slowly, laying him down with care. I kept a hand on Roman the whole time, just shifting my position to give them better access. I was grateful he was out of it when they started the IV because he didn't notice. They moved us to a room, hoping to make Roman more comfortable. Anna's parents left to get some coffee, and I was alone. Everything crashed down on me at once as soon as they were out of the room. Silent tears rolled down my face as I thought about everything the nurses had told us. If Roman hadn't gotten to the hospital when he did, it would have been really fucking bad. I felt like I failed him.

We had been moved into a real room so Roman could rest comfortably in bed. I had been holding his tiny hand for half an hour, still waiting on test results, when Anna rushed in frantically. I stood quickly, not releasing my hold on Roman and reached for my woman. Anna pushed me back, forcing me to let go of Roman's hand, piercing me with rage-filled eyes. I started to ask what the hell was wrong with her when her finger jabbed me in the chest.

"What the hell were you thinking?! You can't just take my boy without me, Noah. He is my responsibility, not yours!" Whisper-yelling at me, her nostrils flared out, her face was red, and her breathing was heavy – in other words, she was pissed the fuck off.

"Anna, you were out like a fuckin' light, babe. He threw up and was cryin' like crazy, and you slept through the whole thing. He needed someone and the whole damn reason I stayed was to help, to take care of him!" I tried to keep my voice low, but it was damn near impossible. I couldn't back down now. She needed to accept that I was a part of their life; I had the *right* to take care of her and Roman.

"Noah, you can't just take over, I would have woken up." Anna's strength was waning, her fever taking over again. She was desperate to believe that she didn't need me – just as desperate as I was to prove she did.

I cupped her face in my hands, holding her with a firm grip when she tried to back away. Looking into her eyes I saw the uncertainty and fear that made her keep me at a distance. It gutted me to know she thought I would hurt her. I understood it, though, after everything Kiersten had said. "Anna, I wasn't taking over anything. I was taking care of you, both of you. That's all I want to do, don't you get it? You two are everything to me."

I felt her lean towards me and took a chance, removing my hands from her face and wrapping my arms around her. I'm pretty sure she thought about resisting, but the day had been too long and she didn't have the strength. I stroked her back in soothing circles and turned slightly so she could rest her hand on Roman. After a minute she finally relaxed and molded her body to me, using one hand to rub Roman's arm and the other on my back. We stood there quietly for a moment while she gathered herself.

"When I got here, the nurses said he was doing better. If this is better, it must have been really bad." I heard her sniff a sharp breath, practically willing herself not to cry.

"The fever is going down, but we are waiting for some tests to figure out what's wrong. All you've really missed out on is cleaning up puke." She responded to my shitty attempt at some humor with a snort and shifted out of my arms. It didn't feel like she was pushing me away, so I allowed her the space. I looked at her – really looked at her – and saw how pale and weak she was. "How are you feeling?"

Before answering, Anna sat in the chair I had been in, sighing loudly as if standing was a chore. I couldn't take it anymore, so I picked her up, sat back down and placed her in my lap. I also put a hand back on Roman, who was starting to stir. I needed to keep touching both of them to stay sane at this point. "Babe, are you doin' alright?"

"I took some more ibuprofen on the way here, and I'm still a little hazy from the other meds, but I'll be fine. I was so scared when Pete finally woke me up. Thank you for taking care of my baby, Noah."

She collapsed against me and wrapped both arms around my neck as her body was racked with sobs. I finally let go of Roman and folded both arms around Anna, giving her the support she needed. Rose appeared in the doorway, but stopped short at the sight of us in the small hospital chair. I could see tears filling her eyes, but she did a hell of a job holding them back. I patted Anna's back and whispered in her ear, "Your parents are back."

She turned to see her Mom just as her Dad came up behind her, never letting go of me. They must have figured Anna would be here soon because each carried two steaming cups of coffee. Her father caught my eye and gave me a heavy stare. It was one of those silent conversations that said more than words ever could.

I pulled Anna in tighter and we waited in silence for some answers. I inhaled deeply, catching the scent of peaches. How she still smelled so damn good I had no idea, but it calmed me in a way that nothing else could. It was a terrible way to come together, but here we were, leaning on each other for support.

Chapter Thirty

Anna

It seemed like hours though it was only moments that I clung to Noah. I forced myself to release him and tried to stand up. I was a little shaky, but starting to feel better. My Mom held out a cup of coffee and I almost cried right then and there in gratitude. Wrapping my hands around it, I moved over to a chair near the small table in the room. I took a few slow sips, careful to not burn myself.

"How did you get here?" I looked up at the sound of his voice to find Noah staring at me with startling intensity. He was still rooted next to Roman; protective, yet tired.

"Pete drove me. He let me out at the ER doors and went to park. He should be making his way up soon." I turned to my Mom, "I saw Max was on shift, so they probably ran into each other."

A smile spread across her face, "Oh good, Max is terrific! I hope Roman is on his patient list." Her eyes went up to the ceiling in thought for a moment. "How long has it been since you saw Max, Banana?"

I wish I could say the blush that spread across my face was from the fever, but that would be a lie. I had had a crush on Max Shaw all through first grade and my family still thought it was hilarious. He had been friends with my brother and was the "cool kid." I looked back up to answer her and saw Noah's face filled with a mixture of interest and anger out of the corner of my eye. I rolled my eyes at him and turned back to my mother. "It's been a while, Mom. I never could get over him, even after he turned me down, so I just constantly avoided him." I saw Noah's jaw tick and smiled to myself. It felt good to have someone so possessive of me. It had been a long time since I was wanted like that.

I gave him a sly smile, "Oh yes, Noah, it was heartbreaking. I begged, pleaded, and cried, but nothing I said would make him kiss me." Noah's mouth dropped open as his eyebrows pulled down into a V. Just as I was about to set him straight, Pete walked in.

"Yup, Noah, it was embarrassing. There she was in pigtails, begging an older man to just give her one kiss. He told her girls had cooties and bolted from the playground." He barked out a laugh and wiped a tear from his eye. "Good thing first grade doesn't last forever, eh sis?"

Noah visibly relaxed, mouthing "You're going to get it" at me with a smirk. Roman stirred just then, calling out for Noah. I tried to tell myself that it was because Noah was the last person he saw, but I knew better. Noah was who he wanted. The man had become like a father to him over these past months. Noah didn't shy away from it, either. He focused completely on Roman, leaning over, close to Roman's mouth so my boy wouldn't have to strain his throat to talk. That's when everything clicked into place. Noah wanted me, the good, bad and ugly – he wanted us. I stumbled over my words for a minute as the epiphany became all-consuming. So what if he had a bitch ex-girlfriend? I was letting her win, letting her come between us. Noah didn't need us to make a family, he could have any girl. He wanted me simply because of who I was. And we needed him – he was the missing piece to our puzzle.

Roman started to sit up, and Noah stood to help me over to his side. I looked at Noah, taking care to show him everything I was feeling. He cocked his head to the side, as if trying to figure me out, until he understood. Noah bent to my ear, he whispered for me only, "We need to talk when we get home, yeah?"

I nodded and let him lead me to the chair at Roman's beside. A few more minutes went by before Max came in. The tests had come back that Roman had come down with stomach flu and now that the fever was under control, he could go home and rest.

An hour and a mountain of paperwork later, Noah drove Roman and me home. Roman sat in the middle of the bench seat with his head on my lap, and I stroked his hair gently. By the time we pulled into the driveway, Roman was asleep. Noah exited the truck and came around to my side. Careful not to disturb him, Noah pulled Roman into his arms and carried him the entire way to his bed. Pete had put clean sheets on before we left, and I thanked God for my brother and his cool head.

Noah moved to go to the living room, but I grabbed his arm and led him to my bedroom. Surprise covered his face, but he didn't question me. Silently he sat down of my bed, waiting for me to speak. My head was finally clear of fever, and I knew it was time to let it go. This was our time.

"I, um, I - thank you Noah, for everything. You were amazing tonight." I started pacing, unsure of how to tell him how I was feeling. Noah just sat there, letting me get my thoughts together, not saying a word.

"I've missed you, you know. Roman has too." My fingers plunged into my hair, "I just, I was scared. I didn't think I could handle it if something happened. It has been so long since someone was in my life; I just didn't know how to handle it. So, instead of talking to you, I shut down, shut you out, and hid myself away."

I stopped pacing now, and knelt in front of Noah, taking his hands in mine. A slow grin appeared, as he spoke, but again I cut him off. "I know we can't start over, what's done is done. But I want to move forward – with you. Can we do that?"

Noah's mouth opened as if to speak, but at the last second he changed his mind and surged forward at me. His lips crashed onto mine as his hands came up behind my head. Need overtook sensibility as Noah pushed up onto his feet, and spun me around, never breaking our kiss. We fell back on the bed; our lips, tongues, and teeth a fury of need. I threaded the fingers of one hand through Noah's hair, pressing him firmly to me, as I slid the other hand underneath the hem of his shirt. Noah shifted his weight, pressing his hard length into my sex.

I moaned into his mouth and he ground down again, more deliberately. A growl came from the back of his throat and he lifted himself up, ripping his shirt over his head and throwing it. Noah's eyes were wild, like he was an addict and I was his drug and it felt good to be craved. I pulled my top off at the same time, then reached up and undid the button of his jeans, pushing them as far as I could without knocking us both over.

Kicking them off, Noah leaned over me, working his thumbs into my waistband. With a sharp tug he ripped my yoga pants and panties to the floor and just froze. His eyes roamed my naked body, worshiping the sight of me. Normally, insecurities would worm their way into my head under such intense scrutiny, but we were far beyond that. I let the heat of his stare sear my skin, and when he did finally touch me my entire body shook with anticipation.

Noah trailed his fingertips up my leg, pausing to make small circles along my inner thigh. I shifted hoping to coax his hand closer to where I needed it. Noah chuckled softly, "Nope, I'm going to take my time. I am going to explore every fucking inch of this body tonight – it's been too long, Anna." To prove his point he placed a knee on the bed and kissed me from my hip bone to my belly button.

His tongue dipped into the indention and swirled around. At the same time, Noah's hands made their way up to my breasts; his thumbs caressing my nipples into tight buds before giving them a slight pinch, sending a shot of electricity throughout my body. My brain shut out everything except the feeling of Noah's body. The heat from his mouth moved up my stomach, leaving me only for a second until he took my right breast into his mouth and sucked hard. I arched my back, forcing myself further into his mouth, and Noah circled his thumb around my clit. The sensations were too much, and I was unable to hold back my moan.

Noah released my breast, "God, Anna, I missed that sound. Hearing how much you want this undoes me." He lowered his head and started on my left breast, his thumb still circling where I needed him most. My core was on fire, wetness dripped from the apex of my thighs and I wasn't sure if I was going to survive our reunion at this point.

I could feel his cock pressing into my leg. I reached down and wrapped my hand around it, finally in control of at least one part of my body. I stroked the velvet covered steel as Noah slowly inserted a single digit into my soaking wet channel. Instantly, the muscles contracted around his finger like a vice. With a whimper of protest from me, Noah removed his finger, only to plunge two back in its place.

I increased my pace on his cock, hoping to increase his tempo to match mine, while grinding into his hand. Noah pressed his mouth to mine with a soft sensuality. He was taking control back, slowing us down. He slowed his fingers, dragging them in and out while his thumb stroked my clit. Noah's tongue mirrored his fingers, and I released his cock, placing my hands on either side of his face.

Noah pulled back and stared at me, still working his magic down below. His eyes were filled with emotion; many of the same ones I was having if I was reading him right. Heat seared my skin as Noah leaned in and kissed his way down my collar bone, chest, and stomach. I mewled in pleasure as his breath blew across my core. Fingers still moving at a tortuous pace, Noah ran his tongue in slow, lazy circles around my clit.

I couldn't stop my hips from grinding against him or my hands from gripping his hair, holding him in place. I was so close; the wave was building higher and higher with each thrust, each lick. I gasped as Noah sucked hard on my clit, plunging his fingers in deep at the same time. The wave crested and pounded through me over and over again – Noah sucked and licked all while dragging his fingers along my walls. The orgasm was the most I ever felt, pulsing around his fingers lasting for what seemed like forever.

Just as I came back down to Earth, Noah spread my knees apart and placed his rock hard shaft at my center, pausing for a split second before impaling me. As my back arched up, he bent down, meeting me in the middle with slow, patient kisses. This was more than make up sex – more than a carnal need for each other. This was Noah and I making love. The words were unnecessary; the feeling was surrounding us, a promise with every touch. We may not have ever had that conversation, but we were having it now. Each movement was a vow, a promise.

My pleasure began to build again, heat and desire filling every muscle. Noah's pace picked up, telling me he was getting close to where I was. Noah released my mouth and gently bit my nipple, pushing me over the edge. As my walls pulsed around him he let go with a groan. He collapsed on top of me, pushing me down into the mattress.

After a minute, he rolled off of me and instantly I missed the contact. I didn't realize Noah had gotten a condom on – in my defense I was extremely distracted – but he was walking to the trashcan while tying it off. I slipped under the covers, lifting the corner as an invitation. I was rewarded with a full smile and a quick kiss before Noah pulled me to him, his arms wrapped around me tightly.

"I'm not leaving, Anna. Don't ask me to because I won't do it." Noah's voice was gravely and serious. This was important to him – he needed this to be sure of what was happening between us. What he didn't know was that I needed it too. I needed to feel him next to me, to understand that he was mine as much as I was his.

"I don't want you to leave." I stated simply. His arms held me tighter for a moment. Just as I thought I would run out of air, he released me slightly and kissed my neck. I turned, pressing my back to his front tightly, so that there was no space between us. Noah pressed his lips below my ear before resting his head on the pillow. It wasn't long before sleep took us.

***

I woke up hours later and stretched my arms. The place that Noah had been was now empty. For a moment my heart sank, thinking he slipped out without a goodbye, but when I heard voices coming from the other side of the door, I laughed at my stupidity.

Dressing quickly, I left my room and headed for the kitchen. I found Noah and Christine at the kitchen table studying some papers laid out in front of them. I hadn't expected Chris to be here – hell I didn't even know where she went yesterday. I raised my hand and gave a little wave, moving towards the counter. I stopped in my tracks when I saw that it was half covered with boxes of pastries from Mrs. Maloney's. I turned around to my sister in confusion.

"I felt terrible that I wasn't here last night. Pete called me this morning and filled me in, so I booked it back here to make sure you were ok." Her eyes slid to Noah who was still looking at the papers on the table and then back to me. "Looks like you're just fine." An evil grin slowly made its way across her face as heat filled my cheeks.

I cleared my throat, hoping to mask my embarrassment, "That was nice of you. Where did you take off to anyway?" How was that for a subject change?

"Smooth, Banana. Ok, well I'll play along. I had a call from a realtor about a place near Charleston I've been looking at. It was late when we got done, so I spent the night with Megan instead of trying to come home. I would have if I had known how bad it would be." The sincerity of her guilt broke my heart.

"Chris, that's not your job. So, I didn't know you were this serious about moving. You know you can stay here as long as you want to." As I was speaking there was a war going on in my head. I never wanted my sister to feel like she had to leave, but if she did, Noah could move in here. The thought stunned me; was I ready for that? Looking to Noah, seeing him fresh from sleep, starting his day with me, yeah that was something I could get used to.

I glanced back to see Christine beaming at me. Knowing she could read my thoughts had me blushing yet again. I went and filled a cup of coffee and grabbed a box of treats to bring to the table. Noah was explaining some of the things he could do with the structure of the house to make it suit her needs better.

"I know I can, Anna, but it's time for me to get my own place, you know? Besides, I feel like it might get crowded soon." She started snickering when Noah looked up at me with a broad, toothy grin. I couldn't help but smile back – I was really looking forward to our future now.

I set the mug and box down and grabbed Noah's cup to refill it. His hand reached up and gave my hip a quick squeeze and then went back to work. It's amazing how after weeks of separation it was so easy to fall into old habits. It all came together in one night – one really stressful, hot, amazing night.

I returned with the coffee and grabbed a raspberry and cheese Danish before settling into a seat. I was taking my first bite when my chair flew sideways, almost throwing me to the floor. I grabbed the edge of the table to steady myself and peered at Noah over my food as I bit into the fruit-filled, sugary goodness. He just laughed at me and shook his head.

"You were too far away, babe."

Duly noted, sit thisclose to Noah – got it. I did my best to glare at him, but he just rolled his eyes and went on about Christine's new house. As they discussed where a patio would be best placed, I began to wonder about what Craig would think about her move – and her not involving him in the remodel discussion. I really didn't know what was going on with them. Christine said they were starting over, as friends, but I knew there was more. I started to say something, but thought better of it, saving it for a private conversation. Instead, I finished my coffee and Danish while listening to their conversation.

"I'm going to go check on Roman, I'll be right back." I slipped out of my chair and made my way to Roman's bedroom door, careful to open it quietly. I sat down gently on his twin bed and placed my hand on his head. It was still warm, but nothing out of control. Satisfied that he was resting comfortably, I went back to my room to dress for the day.

The store would be opening soon, so I took a quick shower and wrapped my still wet hair into a bun. I was exhausted from lack of sleep, but threw on a pair of jeans that did wonders for my ass and a floral print peasant blouse. I checked the time and saw we only had thirty minutes left, so I hurried into the kitchen and got another cup of coffee.

Christine went to her room to get ready, leaving Noah and I alone in the kitchen. I sipped the fragrant coffee at the counter, watching the fine male specimen stand from the table. He took slow, purposeful strides, stopping inches from me. I welcomed the heat from his hands on my waist as he pulled me to him. Moving the cup from his path, Noah gave me a soft, lingering kiss. He took the cup from my hands and set it on the counter, then grabbed my hands and wrapped them around his waist. I couldn't help but smile against his lips.

"What?" He asked with false innocence. "I like having you wrapped around me."

What could I say to that? Nothing, I know. So instead, I pressed my palms into his back, leaving no room between us. His thumb brushed across my nipple, causing me to gasp. Noah used that opportunity to massage my tongue with his, pressing my ass against the edge of the counter.

"Noah!" Roman's joyful shout had us jumping apart like teenagers caught on the front porch. I watched as Noah went to Roman and picked him up cautiously, checking his forehead and cheeks for heat. "You're still here!" Roman must be feeling better; his smile was bright, clearly happy to get extra time with his friend.

Noah looked at me for help and I just tilted my head to one side, shrugging a shoulder, and pressed my lips together. It was up to him how he answered; I was fine with it either way. I saw his eyes soften as understanding dawned on him.

"Well, actually, I spent the night, bud. Is that alright?"

"Course it is. You can share my room if ya wanna." Roman barely contained his excitement. He was more than comfortable sharing our home with Noah. The funny thing was so was I.

"Well, that's real nice buddy, but your bed's kind of small for me. Don't you worry, I'll be ok." Noah ruffled Roman's hair and set him down, helping him pick out something to eat from the mass of baked goods now in the kitchen. "What do you say us guys hang out all day while the girls go to work, yeah?"

Roman's eyes lit up, and he nodded his head furiously, unable to speak. Instead, he wrapped his arms around Noah's legs and hugged him tight before sitting down to eat. Noah sauntered back, resting his hip on the counter.

"I'll take care of him today, don't worry about it. We'll watch a movie, color, all the shit he loves. You just take care of you, yeah?"

"Thanks, Baby." I leaned in to kiss him on the cheek, but stopped when his hands covered my biceps and held me in place. I looked at him, confusion written across my face. "What's wrong?"

"That's the first time."

"First time for what?" What the hell was he talking about?

"That was the first time you called me something other than 'Noah,' babe. We're making progress." He brushed his lips across mine and made his way back to the table. I stood there, stunned for a moment. He was right, though, I had never called him anything but Noah. I didn't usually use cutesy names with anyone outside of my family. And that is what Noah was becoming, part of my family. And now he knew it too.

Chapter Thirty-one

Noah

After Christine and Anna went downstairs, Roman, and I sat at the kitchen table, he was coloring and I was working on some ideas for Craig's neighbor, Mr. Pryor. It was crazy how quickly Roman had recovered – kids are amazing.

"Hey, Noah?" Roman squeaked out, curiosity written all over his face.

"Yeah, Rome?"

"Wha'cha drawin'?"

"Well, the guy that lives next to my friend Craig wants us to make him a sunroom. These are just some ideas I had for him to look at. What do you think?" I knew he was just a kid – a kindergartener – but I really wanted to know what he thought. My Dad had always asked me. At the time I thought he was just being nice, humoring me, but sitting here with Roman, I understood now that he really wanted to hear what I had to say.

Roman's lips pursed and his eyes narrowed as he scrutinized my work. I was shocked to realize I was nervous to hear his answer. It seemed like hours – but was just minutes – before he stood straight, taking his attention from the papers, and cocked his head to one side.

"Why can't he just go outside?"

"Um, what do you mean?"

"I mean, why do you hafta build a room for the sun? It's outside. He can just sit there, can't he?"

I shook my head, laughing on the inside. "Well, what if it's cold, but still sunny? I don't want to sit in the cold, would you?"

He thought for a minute, his head bobbing back and forth. "Naw, guess not. I like this one." His small finger jabbed at the center picture. This idea was more ornate; French doors and decorative windows instead of large, plain panels and a storm door. I had also added some metal edging to go along the roof trim to imitate vines growing. It was my favorite sketch – the one I hoped Mr. Pryor chose.

Pride filled me as I gave a gentle squeeze to Roman's shoulder. "That's my favorite too, Rome."

He looked up at me, eyes shining, simply replying, "Cool."

***

"Found it!" Roman held up a DVD in victory. "Momma hides it 'cause she hates Mikey, but I always find it."

Upon closer inspection I see that it's the original Teenage Mutant Ninja Turtle movie from the early nineties. This kid is so damn cool to hang out with. When he first asked to pick the movie, I admit I was worried. Visions of purple dinosaurs and catchy songs that make you want to stab yourself made me physically shudder. I never should have doubted him.

As I got the movie started, Noah sat next to me on the couch. His face was serious and his eyes searched mine. It took a lot to intimidate me, and never would I have guessed how on edge one five year old could make me.

"Something wrong Rome?"

"Why do you kiss my Momma?"

Oh. Shit. I wasn't sure how Anna might want me to answer him, but I wasn't going to lie. I was in this for the long haul, no matter what. I figured if Roman was okay with what I was going to tell him it would help make it easier for Anna to accept. I took a deep breath and looked him straight in the eye.

"Rome, buddy, this is serious. I am going to tell you something I haven't even told your Momma. Can we keep it between you and me?"

Roman's eyes got wide, and he stretched taller to make room for the air he sucked in. I couldn't tell what that meant. "You want me to keep a secret? From Momma?"

Damn it, this was not going the way I wanted it to. I stared down at the couch. Of course Anna would have made sure he knew not to do that. I should have known that he…

"Cool!"

What? My eyes whipped up, and I found Roman bouncing, eyes glittering with excitement. Okay, maybe this work out.

"Auntie Chris has me keep cool secrets all the time!" He leaned in close and whispered, "She gets me donuts for a snack sometimes." His shoulders pulled up to his ears as he giggled over his "transgressions" while his nose and eyes crinkled in humor.

"She's pretty cool, yeah?" I shook my head at the thought of Christine – what a goof. "Alright Rome, now this is important." We looked at each other, all signs of laughter gone. "Bud, I love your Momma. One day, I want to marry her and make us a real family. Is that okay with you?"

Tears filled Roman's eyes, spilling out and down his cheeks. My heart seized at the sight of his pure, unbridled emotion. I swiped a thumb over his face, removing the tears as best I could. When I pulled my hand back Roman launched himself at me, folding his arms around my neck and squeezing tight.

"You're gonna be my Daddy?" He whispered it right in my ear, shredding any control I had. I hugged him tight before pulling back to soak in the excitement on his face.

"We need to talk to your Momma about it sometime, but you let me handle that. For now, it's time for Turtle Power, yeah?"

"Yeah!"

We settled onto the couch and watched the cheesy movie. Over time, Roman crawled his way on top of me and fell asleep. The medicine I gave him after breakfast was keeping the fever low, but it was still sucking his energy.

I slipped out from below him careful to not disturb his sleep and pulled a blanket up to his shoulders. I wanted to check on Anna and make sure she wasn't over doing it. She didn't get as bad as Roman, but she had been really sick; she needed to take it easy too.

I made my way down the stairs just in time to see Anna start down the hallway to her studio. She didn't see me, so she kept walking while I picked up my pace. As I turned the corner my heart dropped to the fucking floor. I watched her walk by that damn picture of Henry, touch it lightly with the tips of her fingers, and walk through the doorway.

God damned fucking Henry. She still missed him, wanted him. Hell, she couldn't walk by his picture without connecting with it. We had something, Anna and I, but if she kept holding on to this ghost, I was fucked; I would never have all of her. Anger pulsed through me though I didn't know who I was angry with. I could be angry at Henry, but he was the reason we had Roman, so that wouldn't work. Plus, he was dead – gone but not forgotten. I should be mad at Anna for not letting go, for not giving herself to me. I was here! Alive! I wanted to have her completely – just like she had me.

I could have been mad at them, but I wasn't. I was angry at myself. How can I expect Anna to give herself to me when I just got her back? My own stupid choices had pushed her away. The rage dissipated, and I decided that this was my chance to make damn sure she knew what she meant in my life.

I spun around and headed back upstairs. I got to work in the kitchen while Roman slept. Forty minutes later I had chicken quesadillas and salad ready for lunch. Making my way back to the store, I refused to look down that hallway. I might be determined to move forward and be the man that holds Anna's heart, but if I had to see her touch that picture again, I was going to put my fist through the fucking wall.

"Ladies, lunch is ready. You want to come up or do you want me to bring it down?" I twisted my neck around, looking for Anna and her sister. What I did not expect to find was Dick holding Anna's hand. "You should probably let go now." I spat out through gritted teeth, staring him down. The hotelier smirked at me, his touch lingering on Anna's hand longer than necessary.

"Noah, Mr. James was just stopping by to formally order the commissioned piece I proposed. Isn't that nice?" Anna was doing her best to ease the tension in the room, but that little peckerhead wanted more than a piece of art – he was after a piece of ass.

"That's great, babe. Well, I just finished lunch for you two, so why don't you go eat while it's still hot. You should take a break anyway. You were up all night and need your strength." Even though my eyes never left Dick's, I could feel Anna's eyes roll in annoyance. I didn't care – I was fucking annoyed too. From behind me I heard Christine choke back a laugh, amused at my little display of possessiveness. I didn't care who saw it, Anna was mine. End. Of. Story.

"Come on, Anna. Noah's got this under control. Let's go eat and check on Roman." Christine grabbed her hand and pulled her towards the door. As they passed me I snaked my hand around Anna's middle, pulling her into a deep, wet kiss. I released her, holding her steady as she recovered. Her eyes were wide for a second before she narrowed them, telling me that as irritated as she was, she was turned on too.

"You should have more care in how you speak to customers, Mr. Evans. If this is how I can expect to be treated, I may need to go elsewhere for my art." The fucker was threatening me. Hell, he was threatening Anna.

"I just don't like people messing with what's mine, you understand. Was there something else you needed, or were you on your way out?"

Dick raised one eyebrow and smirked at me. "I'll be in touch." The jackass turned to leave, walked to the door and pulled it halfway open before twisting his neck to look at me. "With Anna. I'll be in touch with Anna." With that, he strolled out to his car and left. Yeah, he was not going to be in touch with my Anna.

Fifteen minutes later a couple of older women came in. I was able to convince both of them that they needed a table setting for twelve. It took me some time to wrap it all up and even more time to figure out how to work the cash register. I was just about the beat the shit out of it when I heard the tinkling of Anna's laugh. I looked up to find her with her hand over her mouth, laughing at me.

"Quit laughin' at me and come over here. These lovely ladies have better things to do than watch me make a fool of myself." I tried for exasperated, but the smile that splayed across my face gave me away.

"Oh honey, leave him. We could watch him all day." I raised my eyebrows in surprise at the old lady and barked out a laugh. "What?

You think it was your fine speech about running out of dishes? Young man, your ass made the sale."

Anna was turning every shade of red I could think of trying to hold back her fit of laughter. I walked from behind the counter right up to her and stood bent over, nose to nose. "They're all yours. And you're going to have to pay extra for me to be ogled." I kissed the tip of her nose and turned to the women. "Y'all have a good day." I made my way out of the store and no one would ever get me to admit that I made sure my ass was on display the whole time – did you know swinging your hips is hard work?

I opened the door to the apartment and stopped at the sound of my name. Christine and Roman were talking about me, and I sure as hell wanted to hear what they had to say. I dropped a big one on Roman and I hoped he was really as okay with it as he had said.

"Me an' Noah's got a secret Auntie Chris."

"Well, should you be telling me?"

"He just doesn't want me to tell Momma. It's okay if I tell you. 'Sides, you already told me."

I felt my eyes grow wide and my heart speed up. How the hell had Christine known about my feelings?

"What do you mean, Rome?"

"He loves Momma, just like you said."

"Oh, sugar, I told you so! You could tell just by the way he looks at her."

I grasped the door knob and let it slam, announcing my arrival. Sauntering in the room like I didn't hear a damn thing, I sat down at the table.

"Hey, Rome, how about you take a bath after you get done, yeah?"

Roman looked at me with his brown eyes – identical to his Momma's – and pouted, "Do I hafta?"

"Yeah, bud, you need to. Besides, it will make you feel better. Let's get you your medicine while you're eating, too."

"Hey, Rome," Christine caught his attention as he played with what was left on his plate, "I'll give you your bath before I go back to work if you want."

He jumped down and ran to Christine for a hug. "Thanks, Auntie Chris! You give fun baths." He ran off to his room stripping his shirt off on the way.

I started putting the leftovers from lunch away and thought about Dick and how handsy he was with Anna. Every passing minute had me more enraged than the last. I sat down and glared at Christine.

"I don't like that guy." I winced slightly, feeling bad for spitting the words out at her like that.

"Oh, really? It was so hard to tell." She rolled her eyes at me and took another bite of quesadilla. "You know, I don't either. He needs to accept that Anna's taken, very taken, and move on. I'm pretty sure your, um, display set him straight."

"Well, he better hope so."

Christine shook her head and laughed, "I better get back to work. If you have stuff to do, I'm sure Anna and I will be able to check on Roman. You don't have to stay."

"I'll check with Anna, but yeah, I've got something to take care of. If she's good with me cutting out for a bit, I will." I got up and made my way downstairs.

Chapter Thirty-two

Anna

I was livid. Mr. James just called and decided he needed to go in "another direction." I wanted to blame Noah so much for this, but I knew deep down, Richard had no interest in anything I was offering. What he wanted wasn't on the table. When he had waltzed into the store, I felt his beady little eyes all over me. I was more than happy for Noah to show up when he did – and a little more than turned on at his possessiveness. I imagine women everywhere want to slap me silly, but it was so good to have him stake his claim so blatantly. I was filled with the sense of being wanted, loved, cherished, and even a little powerful – as if he would explode if I wasn't his. And that kiss, oh my. With his strong as steel arm wrapped around my waist and his smooth, wet tongue plundering my mouth I almost forgot about lunch and dragged him into the studio for privacy. Every touch, every look he gave me drove my body insane. Heat spread through me as gooseflesh popped out with each thought of him. My stomach dipped, and my core clenched. Just thinking about Noah had wetness pooling between my legs.

I had been trying to fix the items on the bottom shelf in front of me for five minutes, but I could not focus. I rubbed my thighs together, trying to regain control of myself when two strong, familiar hands grasped my hips. Pulling my ass into his crotch, Noah groaned.

"That is a sight I could walk in on every day for the rest of my life, babe." Noah pressed his fingers into my flesh before releasing me. I missed his heat immediately when he stepped away. "I've got an errand I need to do. Okay if I leave for a bit?"

"Oh, that's fine. It's not been too busy today. And now that I don't have to work on anything for Mr. James, I can trade off checking on Roman with Chris. Where are you going?" I don't know why I brought up the loss of the sale. Yes I did, I was outraged, and I knew Noah would take my side. He would always take my side.

"Don't skip over that, babe. What happened with Dick?" I watched Noah's jaw tick in aggravation. The muscles in his shoulders tensed, stretching the material tight, showing every line. God, this man was gorgeous. I licked my lips, trying to ward off the hunger that was growing from just one look.

Noah cocked his head to the side and smirked. "As much as I want to know what you're thinking about, I want to know what happened."

"That jackass called after you went upstairs. He said 'I don't think your vision will work well with my hotels. I need an artist with true depth and the ability to judge character.' So I told him that I was none too thrilled with *his* character and hung up on him. Stupid prick just wanted to get into my pants."

Noah took two steps and was all but on top of me, "I'm the only one ever getting in those pants again." His head dipped and his nose grazed my ear. I felt his hot breath tickle my neck and my knees started to buckle. Whispering in my ear, Noah continued, "And I'm going to take those pants off, slowly, licking every inch of your skin on the way down. Then I will take my fingers and work your sweet pussy until you come apart in my hands."

A soft moan escaped my lips as Noah's hand landed on my back, pressing us front to front – I wish it was flesh to flesh. I was still exhausted from lack of sleep, but my body was buzzing with anticipation and need.

"Don't worry about him, babe. I'll make you feel better when I get back, that's a promise." I stumbled as Noah moved away from me; my legs barely functioning now. All I could do was nod and watch him walk out the door, smiling.

When Noah was out of sight, I shook my head, desperate to clear it. We had only been tangled up together a few hours ago, but I was ready for more. I had missed being with Noah so much. Our bodies were so in tune to each other, the pleasure was heightened beyond anything I had ever experienced. Clearing my throat, I got back to work, grateful for the customers that came in a few minutes later and the distraction they provided.

I checked on Roman a few times over the next couple of hours, but he was still sleeping. Pete came in and offered to hang out upstairs in case he woke up. I took the time to get some work done in the studio. I made my way down the hall, pausing to reach out to the picture frame before opening the door. I low growl from behind me had me spinning around scared out of my mind. I saw Noah at the end of the hall, and as relieved as I wanted to be, the feral gleam in his eyes made my heart rate spike – and in a different way than the last time I saw him.

Noah stalked down the hallway, his eyes glowing in anger, burning brighter with every step. I walked backwards into the studio, mouth hanging open in shock. Noah stepped over the threshold and slammed the door. I heard my blood roaring in my ears. I had never been afraid of Noah, and as much as I knew he would never hurt me, I was worried about what was going to happen.

"Noah?" The word came out as a croak. My throat tightened in fear as he squeezed his eyes shut and pressed his lips in a thin line. "Noah, what happened?"

"I can't do this, Anna." My heart sank to the floor as I inhaled sharply. He was happy just a few hours ago! He was talking about forever and now he is angry and walking away from me. From us. Oh God, Roman! What the hell happened? The thought of Roman knocked me out of my stupor. My eyes narrowed at Noah, ready to fight for what we had – I was finally willing to let someone in and I would not let him slip away with no answers.

"You can't do what?" I didn't even try to conceal my anger. As I spoke I worried that I was taking something the wrong way. Maybe he had gotten a phone call that upset him and this had nothing to do with me.

His eyes fought back tears, and the sight undid me. He was in pain and I was the cause, but I had no idea what was going on. I softened my voice and stepped toward him. "Noah, talk to me. What's wrong?"

"I can't fight his ghost, Anna. I can't share you with him." Noah hung his head, obviously ashamed of his admission.

Henry. He was talking about Henry, but why? "You aren't sharing me with anyone. Well, other than Roman, but I know what you mean. I am yours, Noah. Only yours." Tears filled my eyes, and I let them fall, hoping by showing my vulnerability Noah would believe me.

"Then why do you have to touch him? Every time you walk by, you touch him!" Noah was shouting now, his pain radiating from his body. It took me a moment to figure out what he was talking about, but when it clicked I almost laughed out loud.

"Noah." He wouldn't look at me; his eyes darted around the room. "NOAH!" I shouted, finally forcing him to focus on me. "It's Roman."

Confusion clouded his eyes as what I said registered, "What? What's Roman?"

"You're talking about the picture outside the door, right?" He nodded, watching me warily. "That is the first picture I have of Roman." The air in the room changed in an instant. Noah's shoulders lowered in relief and he took a step closer to me. I held out my hand to stop him. I turned around and locked the door. There could be no interruptions. It was time to tell him the whole truth. The truth no one else knew.

"Noah, I need to explain something to you. I need you to listen until I'm finished, okay?" He stayed quiet, his eyes piercing me, straight into my soul. I took a steadying breath. I needed to move, I couldn't do this standing still, so I paced back and forth.

"No one knows this. It wasn't a big deal, but it was private for me and Henry." I saw Noah flinch at the name, but I continued. "Henry and I, we loved each other, that's true. But, God why is this so hard?"

"If you don't want to tell me right now, you don't have to. It wasn't fair of me to be so upset." Noah's voice was thick with emotion. He was offering me an out, but I couldn't take it. He deserved to know how I felt.

"No, I need to do this. You need to hear this."

Breathe in. Breathe out.

"Noah, Henry and I weren't in love. We loved each other, but as friends. Henry and I had an arrangement, not a relationship. We kept that to ourselves; I mean, was it really anyone's business? But, then he died. I didn't want my son to wonder if his parents loved each other, or him. So I continued to keep it to myself. It wasn't hurting anyone. Not really. And people left me alone about dating; no one pushes you when you're grieving. I had Roman, and that was all I needed."

I moved to him, needing to feel him in order to stay steady. I laid my hand on his arm and watched his eyes drift from mine to my hand

and back. He didn't make a sound, but there were so many questions in his eyes. Questions that needed answers.

"Noah. What Henry and I had, it wasn't real. It wasn't a love that you dream of." I paused, swallowing my fear. "It wasn't us."

I watched my words sink in. The moment they registered, Noah attacked me. His lips came crashing down on mine. I could taste his need, his desperation for me. My hands instantly dove into his hair and I clung to him like a life line. Noah's hands went to my ass, lifting me. My legs naturally wrapped around him as he walked backwards.

My back slammed into the wall as Noah pressed himself against me. I could feel his thick arousal through his jeans, rubbing against me, forcing wetness to form in my most sensitive area.

I was being lowered to the ground, and before I could protest, Noah grabbed the hem of my shirt and tugged it off. I was frantic by now, ripping his shirt over his head. I craved his skin – I wanted to feel him touch every inch of my body. As I tossed his shirt aside, Noah undid my pants and had them on the floor. I fumbled with his jeans but finally freed him. Pushing his jeans and boxer briefs off in one go, his cock sprung free, making my mouth water.

Without another thought, I hit my knees and licked him from his base to the mushroomed tip. He was harder than I had ever seen him before. The head of his manhood was almost purple – it looked angry. I slid the tip just past my lips and sucked hard.

I heard a guttural sound come from Noah and I pulled him in deeper. Noah's fingers threaded through my hair as he applied the slightest amount of pressure. I sucked and licked, wrapping my hand around what I couldn't fit into my mouth. I reached up and grabbed his ass with the other hand, pushing him into me.

I could feel his hips flex, trying to hold back, not wanting to overtake me. I wanted him to take me, own me. I was his in every way and now he knew it. I pulled him out of my mouth and swirled my tongue around the slit, savoring the salty taste of him.

Without warning, Noah hooked his arms under mine and hauled me up. Again his hands held me up by my ass and again my legs wrapped around him. But this time there was no barrier between us. Noah pressed me against the wall and slid one hand down, stroking my clit and lower lips. I hissed in pleasure and excitement. Noah inserted a single digit into my channel and I could feel my wetness drip out around him.

"Fuck babe, you are so ready for me. I can't wait."

"So don't."

With those words, Noah thrust up into me, causing me to yell out. Over and over he drove into me, each stroke more powerful than the last. His thumb massaged my clit, and I felt my pleasure building, churning within me. Noah dipped his head and with the next thrust he sucked my nipple into his mouth. I shattered into a million pieces, calling out his name. Noah continued his assault, extending my bliss with every movement. As my walls contracted around him, Noah grunted in my ear, "Fuuuuck."

He pressed his forehead against mine with his eyes closed. I could feel him clenching his teeth together and hear him pulling in slow, calming breaths.

"I love you."

Noah spoke so quietly I almost thought I imagined it. I pulled my chin up, forcing him to move his head back so I could see his beautiful face. It was all there in those deep, blue orbs. The last wall, the last line of defense fell apart.

"I love you, too."

Noah kissed me gently, yet with passion, lowering my feet to the ground. He slipped out of me and stepped back. Without a word we gathered our clothes and redressed. We kept stealing peeks of each other until I started to giggle at the silliness of our actions.

We had just had wild, crazy wall-sex and now that we had professed our love for each other, we were acting like teenagers. It was wonderful.

"I got something for you while I was out." I gave Noah a quizzical look, but didn't speak. I was frozen in place. "I wanted to get this a while back, actually, but, well, a lot of shit happened. It hit me fast, but I've known this was right from the very beginning." Noah pulled up his pants and reached in his pocket. I stopped breathing when a small black box appeared in his hand. Noah's full, brilliant smile was blazing at me, loving my reaction.

"Anna Johnston, I love you more than anything. I love your laugh, your smile, your heart. I love your son as if he was my own. Please, tell me you'll be my family, my life. Anna, would you please do me the honor of being my wife?"

Tears flowed freely down my cheeks. I never thought I would find someone so perfect for me. Noah made me happier than I ever thought possible. He loved me. He loved Roman. He was it.

Noah cleared his throat, anxious for my answer. I forced myself to move and placed my hands on either side of his face. I pressed my lips to his softly before answering into them.

"Yes."

Epilogue

Anna

Noah slid the gorgeous ring in place before picking me up by my waist and spinning me around. Laughter filled the studio as we enjoyed our private celebration. My hands were linked together behind Noah's head as I pulled him in for one more passionate kiss. This kiss was a mixture of happiness, passion, and even a little bit of relief.

Noah was mine and I was his – forever. There was one more person we needed to include before I could yell from the rooftops that I was going to marry Noah Evans.

Noah set me on the floor and pressed his forehead to mine. "Are you ready to go upstairs? As much as I want to continue this private celebration and take you up against the wall again, I have to admit that I am nervous thinking about how Roman will react. How about we go upstairs and talk to Roman now and then I take you out tonight so we can pick up right where we left off?"

"Sounds perfect. Let's go." I grabbed Noah's hand and tugged him upstairs. He may have been nervous to see Roman's reaction, but I knew better. In fact, I was pretty sure Roman would be even more excited than the two of us. As I opened the door to the apartment, Noah squeezed my hand and brushed his thumb over the diamond as if to remind himself that I was wearing his ring. A rush of chills went through me at the gesture, reminding me of how close we were to losing this because of my stubbornness and fear.

As we entered the living room, hand-in-hand, we found Pete and Roman watching that damn turtle movie – again. I grabbed the remote to turn the television off and moved out of the way of a flying pillow courtesy of my dear brother.

"C'mon Banana! It's the best part; you can't turn it off right now." Pete's eyes glittered in amusement until they skimmed down my arm to my hand. His eyes widened for a split second before a huge, genuine, and happy smile spread across his face. "You know what, Roman? I think we need some snacks. Let's pause the movie while I run out and get some for us."

Roman's face screwed up in annoyance and he was just about to tell my brother what he thought of that plan, when Pete chimed in one more time, reminding me of how amazing a man he truly was. "Hey, I have an even better idea, Bud. What do you think about us letting your Momma and Noah go out tonight, alone? I'll go get something to make for dinner while your Momma says whatever it is she needs to say. Does that work for you?"

Roman mulled over his answer for a moment, "Do we get to see the rest of the movie, Unca Pete?"

"Yeah, and we'll even watch the second one too." Peter stood up from the couch and walked over to me, wrapping me up in a bear hug before he whispered in my ear. "I am so happy for you, Banana. You deserve this. You both do. Text me when I can come back, and then you two can have this night to yourselves, ok?"

I looked at my brother, really looked at him, and saw relief and love throughout his face. Pete had seen me through so much and never asked for anything in return. I smiled at him and gave him another squeeze before he released me, letting me step back. "Thank you, Peter. You are my favorite brother."

With that, he tweaked my nose and walked over to Noah, clapping him on the back and shaking his hand. They leaned their heads together for a quick conversation that ended when both men threw their heads back laughing. Roman observed the whole scene in confusion, unsure of what everyone was so happy about. He watched Pete walk away and disappear through the doorway before glancing at us, knowing he should ask a question, but not sure what that question was.

"Hey, Rome, Noah and I need to talk to you. This is really important, alright?"

He nodded his head slowly, his eyes shifted back and forth between Noah and me. Noah sat on the couch next to my son – our son – and put his hand on Roman's small shoulder. The sight of the two of them together made my heart skip a beat and warmth flow through my entire body. This was right, our family was whole.

"Roman, do you remember what we talked about earlier today?' I looked at Noah puzzled by his question. Roman, on the other hand, just nodded his head vigorously at Noah, his eyes wide. "Well, it didn't take as long as I thought it would."

I watched as the pieces clicked together in Roman's head and understanding dawned. I hadn't known the exact discussion had been, but it wasn't hard to figure out now. The fact that Noah had taken the time to talk about our future with Roman was just one more reason to love him.

Roman launched himself off of the couch and into my arms, wrapping his arms around my neck and slapping a wet, noisy kiss on my cheek. He buried his face in my neck and I could feel his tears dripping onto my skin. His voice was muffled, so I almost missed it when he whispered to himself, "I'm gonna have a Daddy."

Tears rolled down my face as I motioned to Noah. He knelt down on the floor and wrapped his strong arms around both of us. We stayed there for a few minutes, just enjoying the feeling of togetherness, until the door slammed open and Christine ran in, shrieking.

"Let me see it! Let me see!" The room erupted in laughter as Noah grabbed Roman and gave him a bear hug while Christine held onto my hand so hard I started to lose the feeling in my fingers. We still had to tell my parents, but right now I just wanted to live in the moment. I was happy, truly happy, for the first time in a long time. I felt like every scar and every hurt was healed, and I could begin to live again.

The End.

Rachel Caid

Acknowledgments

I would like to thank some of the people that helped me create the world that Anna and Noah live in. It's not long, because I tend to hold my emotions close, but I needed to let the world know a little about some of the amazing people in my life.

I absolutely, without a doubt want to express to everyone how amazing my husband has been through this entire process. Sweetheart, you are my everything and without your encouragement, love, and occasional (needed) reality checks, I would never have been able to bring Anna and Noah's story to life.

Nicky Crawford, holy smokes girl, you are amazing!! All of the time and effort you put into helping me refine this work was above and beyond anything I could have imagined. I am truly grateful to have found a friend like you. Your books are going to rock the indie world :)

Ella Stewart, you, omg, YOU! You have given me peace, support, courage, connections, and most importantly, you have given me a book bestie that I will cherish for freaking ever! Thank you for helping me keep my head on straight and for being available every time I wanted to freak out.

Kristi Webster, thank you so much for such a fantastic cover! I am so glad we went in the abstract direction we did. Those late night chats (with the most awesome pottery images lol) were so much fun. I cannot wait to work with you on Eyes Open.

My beta readers, you ladies rock my socks. Your support and honesty made a huge difference in not only my book, but my life.

To my readers, I am so grateful for the time you took to read Anna and Noah's story. I hope you enjoyed their journey and I look forward to you seeing what's in store for Christine and Craig.

About the Author

Rachel Caid lives in Missouri with her husband and two sons. She is a self-proclaimed coffee addict with no plans on recovery and an avid reader of all types of romance. Her day job is very black and white, so she enjoys being able to lose herself in the colorful world on novels; whether it's reading or writing them.

Find her at: http://www.facebook.com/authorrachelcaid

Coming Soon

Eyes Open (Finding Home Series book two)

Christine has a secret she's hidden from everyone for years.

Craig struggles with his desire for Christine and the need for full disclosure.

Boundaries will be tested.

Lives will be altered.

Will love overcome?

Made in the USA
Charleston, SC
27 October 2015